MYTHICAL ALLIANCE

PHOENIX TEAM

USA TODAY BESTSELLING AUTHOR
CLAIRE LUANA

The guy at the bar wasn't my type. He was human, for one.

He threw back a shot as he and his buddy ogled the ass of a passing blonde. Strike two. He was stocky and thickly muscled on top—whereas I preferred a man lean and strong. Proportioned as nature intended. Strike three. Sad little goatee and too-tight Ed Hardy T-shirt. Strikes four and five.

It didn't matter. I was still going to go over there and pick him up tonight.

Because this ass-hat had something I needed.

I sucked in a breath, swallowed the rest of my bourbon, and stood, fluffing my dark curls up and tugging the neckline of my fitted dress down to show a bit more of my generous cleavage. Too obvious maybe. But was there such a thing as too obvious with guys like this?

I sauntered over to the bar, closing my sensitive glands to the overwhelming power of the man's Axe body spray.

I sidled in next to him and he turned to regard me.

"Buy me a drink?" I smiled widely at him.

He blinked twice as he took me in but only recoiled slightly. I had to give it to him. Most people stuttered or downright stared when they caught sight of my green slitted pupils and curved fangs. I supposed a man who worked security for MASC, the Mythical Alliance of Supernatural Creatures, the UN division governing all things supe, would have gotten used to a strange face every now and then.

His gleaming eyes drank me in. "Those scales go all the way down, honey?"

His skinny friend choked on his beer.

I let my hand drift to my neck, where a pattern of golden scales curved up to my temple. "Buy me that drink and maybe you'll find out." They did, in fact, go all the way down. And he would not, in fact, be finding out.

He grinned and I fought the urge to punch him in his tiny little teeth. "What are you drinking?"

"Martini?" I simpered. I lowered my voice half an octave. "Dirty."

His smile widened and he flagged down the bartender to order me my drink.

The friend stood, grabbing his beer. His eyes

hadn't left me, and even with my glands closed, I could smell his fear. "I'm going to grab a round of pool, bro."

I waggled my fingers at him as he left before sliding onto the stool he had just vacated. Fine by me. I didn't need that one screwing up my plans.

A dirty martini was deposited in front of me and I picked it up. "What are we drinking to?" I asked.

He'd ordered himself another shot. The cinnamon tickled my glands. Fireball. The official drink of ass-hats. Or was that Jägermeister? He held up his glass. "To scales that go all the way down."

I giggled and took a sip, nearly gagging. I hated olive juice. But a dirty martini seemed like the type of drink a seductress version of myself would order.

"What's your name?" he asked.

"Veronica," I lied. This jackass deserved nothing real from me. "You?"

"Martin." We shook hands. "Your hands are as cold as ice."

I smiled. "Cold-blooded."

Martin's dark eyebrows shot up like two bushy caterpillars. "What are you?"

Rude. Didn't this guy know anything? You didn't ask a supe what kind of creature they were.

"Naga," I answered. "Well, half anyway." All right, I supposed I'd give him one true thing. Many mythical creatures—supes, as they're called these days—share kinship or at least a passing resemblance with animals. Nagas are snake supes. In ancient times, they were thought to be gods, and that suited them just fine. Nagas are capable of shifting between the form of a human and the form of a huge snake—or somewhere in the middle— human torso, snake lower half. Full-bloods have incredible power—they're strong, fast and agile. All their senses are heightened, and they have an extra one too: nagas can use their infrared glands to sense the heat of a nearby body one hundred yards away. Then there's the poisonous venom, and the fact that nagas can swallow someone whole. Though it isn't a particularly pleasant experience, from what I've heard. You're bloated as hell for days afterwards.

As a half-blood, I can't do most of that cool shit. My form is permanently stuck somewhere between a snake and a human. I have the slivered pupils and forked tongue of a naga, together with a pattern of golden scales that stretch up my neck to my temples as Martin so classily observed. I have much of my race's heightened senses: strength, speed, and venom. But compared to many supes, I'm weak.

His face went thoughtful. "I knew another naga once. At the office."

My gut tightened with anger as tears pricked my eyes. Impotent fury and soul-sucking grief, my two ever-present companions these past six weeks. I took a gulp of martini to hide my reaction, focusing on the disgusting tang of the olive juice. "You don't say," I managed.

Martin sipped his Fireball. "Well, he's dead now. Too bad. I liked the guy."

Me too, Martin. Me too. I wanted to slide off the stool into a puddle of myself. I wanted to rip his head off for even mentioning my dad, for thinking he knew anything about him when this useless human didn't even deserve to live in the same universe. But I'd tried rage, and I'd tried grief. Today, I was trying something new.

Action.

I set my drink down and dropped my hand to his hairy forearm. "Do you want to get out of here?" I could feel the clock ticking down, my ability to hold it together slipping through my fingers like sand through an hourglass. Tonight was the longest I'd been out of the house in weeks. The longest I'd carried on a conversation. The first time I'd showered in...well...it was probably best not to think about that.

"Fuck yeah," Martin replied, throwing back the rest of his shot and standing up.

"Great."

He dropped some cash on the bar and slung a beefy arm around my shoulders. The feel of him made my skin crawl, but I wouldn't have to stand it much longer.

We stumbled out of the bar into the warm night. I

was taller than him, so there was an awkward angle to his arm and our stride. We started down the sidewalk and I caught sight of an alley.

Perfect.

"I don't want to wait," I said as breathily as I could, shoving him into the alley.

"Me, either, baby," he said, and pinned me against the wall, his hands cupping my ass. His liquor-breath was heavy as he crushed his lips against mine.

Oh, Martin, you are so predictable.

I had my first kiss—a human boy named Ryan—when I was thirteen. That was when I learned that it was pretty hard to kiss a human without my fangs getting into the mix. And the deadly poison they excreted. Ryan had ended up in the emergency room and I'd ended up with the tongue-lashing of the century from Dad. Needless to say, Ryan and I did *not* become boyfriend and girlfriend.

But right now, that was exactly what I was looking for. I surged against Martin's mouth and felt my fangs tangle in his tongue, pricking him. His body tensed and he froze, his eyes going wide, his pupils dilating.

"What—" His hands slid off me and flew to his chest. The venom was coursing into his bloodstream now. It would immobilize him, and if left untreated for more than fifteen minutes, would send him into cardiac arrest. "Don't worry, Martin," I sneered as I fished into his back pocket for his wallet. "It's not personal. Oh, wait. Yes, it is." I kneed him in the balls and he fell to the damp pavement with a wheezing groan.

I flipped through his wallet, desperately searching.

Please be here, please be here, please say this wasn't all for nothing...Yes!

His United Nations keycard, which provided access to all the secure levels of the MASC building. My ticket to the answers I needed. I pulled a card duplicator I'd bought on eBay out of my clutch and quickly scanned the card, duplicating it on one I'd made up with my own picture and fake identity.

I put the card back in the wallet and pulled his cash out, shoving it in my purse, before dropping it on his chest. Best if it looked like a simple mugging gone wrong.

I knelt over him, fisting his ridiculous T-shirt in one of my hands to pull him closer. "That naga who died, Martin? The one men like you were supposed to keep safe? He was my father. And he was worth a hundred of you, you stupid piece of shit." I didn't know why I was talking to him; he was totally out of it from the venom.

I stood, looking down at him. His color was leeching away as his vital organs shut down. I had a syringe of anti-venom in my purse, ready to bring him back. But I was stalling. Why? I wasn't a killer. I valued human life. I'd been going to med school, for God's sake, before I'd washed out two months from graduation. But I just couldn't bring myself to care. Why did this worthless douchebag get to live when Dad was dead?

Tears blurred my vision and I felt the despair closing in around me, cloying and suffocating. I didn't fight it. My hourglass had run dry.

The tears came unbidden now.

I was so tired.

So tired and heavy. I eyed the cobblestones beneath my heeled shoes, overcome by the urge to lie down and curl into myself in this filthy alley.

Some distant part of me spoke. *Move.*

Give him the anti-venom. Walk out of here and call an Uber.

One shot. Ten steps. Three taps of my finger.

I could do that.

I turned to find someone standing in the mouth of the alley. Three women, all clad in sparkly dresses and platform heels. Looking at the unmoving body on the ground behind me.

"Oh my god! Is he okay?"

2

———————

F*uck.*

Adrenaline burned through the fog of my grief, leaving the bright sun of panic. There weren't supposed to be witnesses. It didn't look good if I was found robbing and shooting up some guy in an alley...

The morose, self-destructive part of me pushed back. What the hell did it matter if I ended up in prison? My life had already gone to shit. Dad was gone, my medical career was over, I'd been living on cold DiGiorno pizza and boxed wine since Dad's funeral. That was no kind of life. But...a single thought shot through me, blazing bright. If I went to prison, I'd never find out who'd killed Dad. I'd never be able to avenge his death. It was enough to keep me going. That one shining purpose. After that, it was anyone's guess.

Damn it, I needed to save Martin.

"My date's gone into some sort of anaphylactic shock!" I cried. "I think he ate something he's allergic to! Call 911!"

One of the women, a brunette in a tight red dress, fished into her sequined clutch. "I have an EpiPen!"

Seriously? Those were some fucking odds. Well, hitting him with a jolt of epinephrine likely wouldn't hurt. "Help him!" I motioned her into the alley, crouching down next to Martin and quickly hiding his wallet beneath him. His skin had gone pale and waxy and his lips were tinged blue.

"This has never happened before." I played the helpless waif. "Where do we put it in?"

The brunette knelt down in her stilettos and jammed it into the side of his thigh like a meat thermometer in a turkey. I couldn't help but be impressed by her bedside manner. Cool in an emergency.

Martin's eyes went wide as he took a deep breath, one hand clutching his chest.

"I called 911," one of the other girls said, waving her phone. "An ambulance is on the way."

"Great." I tried to muster some enthusiasm. I needed this girl out of the alley so I could give him the anti-venom. This was going south faster than a sorority girl on spring break.

We helped Martin into a sitting position and I looked at her sideways. "Will you go see if the ambulance is coming yet?" I guessed I looked pathetic enough because she put a hand on my shoulder to comfort me. "He'll be okay."

She hurried back to her gaggle of friends, her heels clicking on the pavement.

I quickly pulled the syringe of anti-venom out of my purse and shoved the sleeve of his T-shirt up, injecting him. His color started returning instantly, his eyes clearing.

"What happened?" he groaned.

"Not all guys can handle their supes," I replied, praying that he didn't remember what I'd said about my dad. Naga venom had mind-altering effects, and he'd already been sinking when I'd spoken to him. I should be okay.

Flickers of red lights along the alley wall joined the whoop-whoop of a siren. "Ambulance is here!" the brunette announced.

The paramedics swarmed the alley and I stepped back, letting them go to work. An ache filled me as I watched their efficient motions. I was supposed to do that. Save lives. I'd wanted to be a doctor since I'd been ten years old. And I'd fucked it up.

They got Martin on a stretcher and into the ambulance. I followed them to the sidewalk, my arms crossed tightly over my chest.

"You coming with?" the paramedic asked. "Let's go."

I held up a hand to protest, but the EpiPen woman motioned me forward. "Go with him!"

"Yeah, go! He'll want you there." The other women joined in the guilt trip and I found my feet moving towards the back doors of the ambulance.

I stepped up into the vehicle, unable to believe that I was being bullied by a pack of party girls. What the hell had become of me?

The space in the back of the ambulance was suffocating. The two paramedics focused on Martin, checking his vitals, talking to him in low tones. They ignored me, which was just fine. As soon as we reached the hospital, I was fucking out of there.

The trip wasn't long, and I stepped out first to let them get the stretcher down. I trailed them into the emergency room as they whisked his stretcher away.

I let out a sigh.

He was gone.

It was over.

I reached for my purse to grab my phone and froze. It was still in the ambulance. I hurried back outside, but the vehicle was gone.

"Shit!"

I spun on my heel and ran back in, up to the front counter. "The ambulance. Where did it go? I left my purse in there. It has all my things..."

The portly middle-aged lady behind the counter pursed her lips, making it clear she had more pressing concerns than my lost handbag. "Which company was it?"

"What?"

"What did it say on the side of the ambulance? We contract with half a dozen providers in addition to EMS."

My mouth opened and closed as I tried to remember, to bring up the ambulance in my mind's eye. Nothing. "I don't know," I admitted.

"Then you're going to have to try each of the companies separately. They're independent from the hospital. We should get a bill within two days and could narrow it down for you then."

"Two days?" I sagged against the counter as I realized how much I had completely fucked up. In addition to my phone, keys, and wallet, my purse contained a used vial of anti-venom, the illegal card reader and the fake UN keycard with my face on it. *Fuck.* If anyone fished around in it...

I slumped on the counter, dropping my forehead to my arms. This night was a disaster. Why had I thought I could do some sort of 007 shit and find out who'd killed Dad? Like I'd ever actually successfully break into the UN and steal their classified report on the events surrounding his death. I'd fucked up every other part of my life; why had I thought this would be any different?

"Honey, you can't just stand there. I have other people to help."

I raised my heavy head. How was I supposed to get home? I didn't even have money for the subway. "Do you have a phone I can borrow?"

With a long-suffering sigh, the front desk lady showed me into an empty patient room. I thanked her and stared at the phone on the wall. I knew exactly three numbers by heart. One was my dad's. The second was my Auntie Temsula's, but she lived in New Jersey. Plus, I seriously didn't want to drag her into this. So I dialed the third number.

It went to voicemail, as I'd expected. No one picked up an unknown number these days.

A cheerful message answered. "*Hi. You've reached Kiki's phone. Leave a message. If you're a telemarketer, take me off your list or I'll make sure your personal data is blasted across the dark web like Halley's Comet. Have a great day!*"

A smile ghosted its way across my lips. Oh, Keeks.

Beep.

"Hey. It's Zariya. It's a long story, but I'm at New York Presbyterian Hospital and could use a ride home. I'm okay. Call me back at this number."

I hung up and waited about forty-five seconds. Long enough for her to listen to the message and call me back. Kiki was never far from her phone.

I picked it up on the first ring.

"Ohmygod, Zariya, are you okay?"

Kiki had been my best friend since we were

eleven, and we'd lived together with our other room-mate, Alviya, in a cramped apartment in Murray Hill for the last two years. She was one of the most talented hackers, excuse me, *computer prodigies*, I knew.

She could also read minds.

Kiki had taught me how to protect my thoughts, and I dropped what was left of my ragged mental walls, letting it all tumble out. I knew my thoughts were loud, jumbled. I didn't care. Kiki's gift worked even over distances, so long as she had a strong personal connection to her target or was connected by technology. And I didn't have the energy to explain right now.

"Oh, Zar..." She made a little *tsking* sound with her tongue. "I'll be right there."

"Thanks."

I WAS SITTING on the sidewalk, my back to the brick wall of the hospital, when Kiki's Uber pulled up half an hour later.

She was wearing cute checked pants, platform black combat boots, and a Pusheen T-shirt. Her short, dark hair was pulled into a spiked ponytail, revealing her side-shave. Kiki had always had way more cool than me.

Her heart-shaped face was clearly worried as she

settled down next to me on the ground. "What's wrong with the bench?" She nodded to an empty bench a few yards away.

"I don't deserve a bench." My words were flat.

She wrapped her arms around me and pulled me into a side hug, comforting me with her tiny body.

"I fucked up so bad."

"I hacked into the dispatch on the way here. Your purse should be headed back to EMS Station 10. We'll get it tomorrow."

Relief welled up in me. "What would I do without you?"

"Run out of DiGiorno pizzas?" she said with a grin. "Frankly, I'm just glad to see you out of the house and dressed in... Are these real clothes? Even if it was to execute an ill-planned heist."

I snorted.

"You just couldn't let it go, could you?" Her words were soft. She knew everything thanks to her supe heritage. Kiki was a satori, a mind-reading supe of Japanese descent. She looked human, but that brain of hers...it was anything but.

"You said you wouldn't get the report for me, so I had to find a way to get it myself."

She leaned back. "And you thought nearly killing some MASC security guy was the way to do it?"

"We're not all super-hackers," I shot back. "Some of us have to use the resources at our disposal." The pitiful, sorry excuse for resources.

"Was this guy with your dad when..." She trailed off. No need to finish the sentence. When he'd died.

"No, he's just some dude. He works out of Turtle Bay." If I'd had access to any of the security guys who'd been on my dad's protection detail, I wouldn't have rolled up with anti-venom, that was for damn sure. But most of them were out of country, working out of the offices in Turkey, where Dad had died.

Kiki pinched the bridge of her nose.

I felt a lecture coming on.

"Z, your dad wouldn't want this for you. He'd want you moving on with your life. I understand it was too hard to finish your last semester and study for your boards after he died, but...you put so much time and energy into becoming a doctor. Haven't you at least talked to Cornell about whether you could come back and graduate? This energy—you have to funnel it into something productive. It's what he would have wanted."

"I can't," I choked out. "I can't think of anything except him lying there, so...still. You knew Dad—he was tough as fucking nails. He was Special Forces for a *decade*. And I'm supposed to believe he was in the wrong place at the wrong time? That some unstable building just happened to tumble over and land directly on his SUV? It's bullshit." I jammed the heels of my hands into my eyes, as if I could hold the tears in. "I've tried to let it go, but I just...can't."

Kiki was quiet for a long time while I cried.

"Okay," she finally said. "I'll do it."

I looked up, sniffling. "What?" The MASC report detailing Dad's death had been classified. I'd begged Kiki to get it for me, but she'd firmly refused.

She let out a long breath through her button nose, flaring her nostrils. "I said I wouldn't get you the report because I thought poring over it endlessly wouldn't help you. But maybe I was wrong. You clearly aren't letting it go. Maybe you need to see it. For closure."

"Yes," I whispered. "For closure." I was afraid to say anything else, for fear that she'd change her mind.

"Okay then." She tucked a lock of hair behind my ear. "Tomorrow we'll get your purse and the report."

A fresh wave of tears flooded over my cheeks. This time, tears of gratitude. I might have lost Dad, but I still had people who loved me. My Auntie. Kiki. Alviya. Why was it so hard to remember that sometimes?

Kiki stood, offering me her hands. "Let's go home."

3

I slept fitfully and woke with a tight headache squeezing at my temples.

I dragged myself into the shower. Twice in two days—a new post-funeral record.

The shower's hot water ran over me until the snake in me cried out for cool. It was a sonofabitch to rely on external temperature regulation. Being a warm-blooded human would be so much easier.

I wrapped the towel around myself and stood on the cool tile. My reflection was blurry in the foggy mirror, but my scales were visible, glittering in the fluorescent bathroom light. I'd always been perched in the middle—not truly human, not truly supe. The only place I'd ever really fit had been with Dad. He'd had a way of filtering out the rest of the world; it hadn't mattered what anyone thought so long as he was proud of me. He'd always been a shelter to me. And now I was alone. Exposed.

"Zariya, you better slither your ass down here or your bagel is mine!" Alviya hollered up at me. She was remarkably peppy for a valkyrie, and I'd been avoiding her sunny presence since Dad had died. Two weeks in, she'd announced that she knew what I was doing and it would only make her try twice as hard to bring me back to the land of the living. She'd shown remarkable perseverance.

Today, for the first time, I found I didn't mind. Perhaps it was actually going outside yesterday, or maybe it was the prospect of finally getting the report... but I thought I'd be able to face her relentless enthusiasm.

I threw on a pair of old jeans and an oversized White Snake T-shirt—a gag gift from Alviya's boyfriend, Basirou, and headed downstairs, threading my thick dark curls into a braid.

A toasted bagel smeared in cream cheese and lox was poised between Alviya's perfect white teeth. Upon seeing me, she set it down on a plate and held it out to me. "You want?" After a year of rooming with her, I was used to Alviya's cavernous appetite. And her feathered wings—downy white as a snowy owl's, strong as an eagle's. The black caverns of her eyes, deep as the pit of Naraka... I wasn't sure I would ever truly get used to those. Even though I loved her like a sister, they were eerie as hell.

I eyed the bagel as a knock sounded on our door.

"That must be Bas. Come in!" she hollered.

The door opened to reveal a dark shadow filling the space. Wings, muscle, towering bulk. "I brought Starbucks!" Basirou stepped inside and flicked the door shut with his tail.

"You darling beast." Alviya retrieved the tray from him and gave him a ravishing kiss. Seeing the two of them side by side used to give me pause. Basirou was a seven-foot-tall gargoyle—ebony skin like dark marble, his wings membranous like a bat. Twisting horns protruded above an unfairly handsome face. Where he was dark, Alviya was fair, with her white wings, creamy pale skin, and bright copper hair. Where his muscles were roped like a Greek statue, she was as lean and long-legged as a ballet dancer. But they were actually good together. I supposed there had been stranger pairs.

"Chai latte for Zariya, Americano for you, some ridiculously sweet unicorn Frappuccino for Kiki that I nearly lost my man card ordering, and a flat white for me." Bas passed out his bounty, then cocked his head at me. He was always too discerning for his own good. "Good to see you up and around, Zar."

"Thanks." I took a sip of the latte, letting the warm liquid soothe me. He'd even gotten it with coconut milk, how I liked.

"What are you up to today?" Alviya asked me.

I shrugged, taking another sip. "The world is my

unemployed oyster." A thought struck me. "Maybe I'll go see Dad."

Bas's dark brows knit together. "You sure that's a good idea?"

Kiki breezed into the kitchen, grabbing her Frappuccino off the counter. "Anything that gets my girl out of the house in real pants counts as a good idea."

"Har har."

Bas chuckled. "Suppose that's true."

"What about you guys? Anything wild and crazy at work today?" Alviya and Bas had met working at a PR company that focused on supe-run businesses and products.

Alviya hoisted her Americano in a faux salute. "You know us, saving the world one selkie sunscreen at a time."

I managed a smile.

"All right, we're out," Bas said with a little wave. "Have a good day."

Alviya and Bas angled themselves out the door, folding their wings to get through the opening. I loved them dearly, but those wings took up a lot of space. The apartment felt three times bigger with them gone.

Kiki turned to me. "I talked to the EMS guys. You can pick up your purse anytime after noon today."

"Thanks, Keeks," I said, waiting.

We looked at each other for a moment before she sighed. "I got the report."

My eyes fluttered closed. Finally.

When I opened them, she was gone, but she returned quickly with a manila envelope. I reached for it eagerly, but she tucked it behind her back. "Before I give this to you, you need to promise me something."

"Anything." I would promise her my firstborn in exchange for that report. Not that there'd ever be a firstborn, at the rate my life was turning into a dumpster fire.

"If you read this, and there's nothing there to find...you gotta let it go. Your dad was the most bad-ass supe I've ever known too, but even he was mortal. Accidents happen. Shitty things happen to good people. I need to know that you'll be objective about this. If there's nothing...just lay it to rest."

I pursed my lips together. I didn't want to let it go. I didn't want to believe a stray pile of bricks could take out my dad where terrorists and armed insurgents had failed.

But Kiki was right. I needed to read what was really there, not what I wished was. "I promise."

She handed it over and I cradled the envelope to my chest. "Thanks." I turned to go back up the stairs to get my shoes.

"You're not going to read it? After all of that?"

"I'm going to read it with Mom and Dad."

My FATHER HAD BEEN full naga, born in the remote eastern corner of India, in Nagaland. I'd never been there. Auntie always told me it was a backwards and boring place, which was why she'd followed Dad when he'd left.

My mother had been human. A grad student accompanying her professor on an anthropological expedition. According to Auntie, the chemistry between my parents had been instant. According to Dad...well, he'd never spoken of Mom at all.

But there must have been some connection, because before they knew it, Mom was pregnant, and he'd accompanied her to America. Interspecies relationships weren't forbidden under the terms of the International Treaty on the Recognition and Protection of Supernatural Creatures (or just the Treaty, as we all called it), but they were frowned upon for all number of reasons. Religious intolerance, xenophobia... practicality. The human body wasn't designed to bear a naga child. As my parents well found out. Auntie said it was a miracle I'd survived. Mom wasn't so lucky.

Her gravestone had been here at Calvary Cemetery in Queens for as long as I could remember. Auntie would take me here on my birthday each year, which had felt like a morbid tradition, but she'd said it was important to honor Mom's sacrifice. As I'd grown older, I'd come to see there was a certain sweetness in that. Dad had never come with us; Auntie had said it was too hard for him.

Now, I wished I'd asked him why. Asked him about her. There were so many things I wished I'd asked him, but I'd been too chicken-shit. And now he was gone.

I stopped before two ebony headstones, hers weathered with age, his new and polished to a sheen. *Vizol Chanji*, it read. *Father. Warrior. Friend.* He was so much more than that, too, but everything my father was couldn't fit in this little space.

The flowers laid on his grave were shriveled and dry, and so I gathered them up, tossing them in a nearby trashcan. When I returned, I shoved my hands in my pockets. "Hi, Mom. Dad. I hope you guys are doing good. Getting reacquainted." My parents had only had a year together—I liked to imagine they were hanging out in the afterlife. Hopefully, they still had something in common. Me, at least.

I sat down, leaning my back against Dad's headstone. It was weird, thinking he was beneath me. Naga tradition dictated that a warrior be cremated after he or she died, but Dad's will had said he'd wanted to be buried beside my mom. I'd often wondered if his stony silence on the subject of Mom meant he'd forgotten her, but with that one action, I knew he hadn't.

I tilted my head back against the hard stone and closed my eyes. "I really fucked up since you left, Dad. It's just too hard..." The words tangled on my tongue. "It's too hard without you here. This isn't how it was supposed to be." He was supposed to be at my med school graduation, supposed to harp on me for working too much during residency, supposed to celebrate with me when I got that cardiac fellowship I'd been eyeing.

A choked laugh escaped me.

"The truth is, everything I did was to make you proud of me. To live up to your legacy. And now that you're gone, it just seems pointless."

Dad had always been larger than life. When he'd come to the U.S., even as an immigrant who hadn't spoken a lick of English, he'd charmed everyone. Nagas were warriors, and so he'd joined the Marines special supe division, rising up the ranks quickly. He'd been recruited for the Force Recon division, where he'd stood out even more, eventually leading his own team. He'd retired almost ten years ago to go work for MASC as a diplomat and consultant. Another distinguished career. Whatever Dad had touched had seemed to turn to gold. Except me, apparently.

I looked at the envelope. I didn't know why I was delaying after I'd been dying to get my hands on the report for the past six weeks.

I tore the envelope open.

I sped through the seven-page report once before

turning back to the front page to read it again, slowly. I needed to take it apart piece by piece. Because there was something here that MASC leadership had missed. I knew it. There was something here that proved that Dad had been murdered. And it was up to me to find it.

4

———

I pulled the report out and read it again on the subway. As if a fifth readthrough would magically help me find what I was looking for. According to the writeup, Dad had been visiting Syrian refugee camps on the Turkish border, checking on the treatment of supes and ensuring UN and MASC supplies were being appropriately distributed. He was traveling in an armored SUV with a Humvee military escort. The three-mile trip from town had been uneventful. The visit to the camp had been uneventful. But on the way back, just two blocks from his hotel, a condemned building three stories high had collapsed into the street. Directly onto my father's caravan. He'd been killed instantly.

MASC had conducted a full investigation. They hadn't uncovered any unusual activity, any sign of explosives or tampering. The building had been bombed in a terrorist attack the year prior and had become structurally unsound. Just an unfortunate accident. Wrong place, wrong time.

Bullshit.

I shoved the papers back in the envelope, drumming my fingers on the subway pole. They must have missed something. There must be *something* on the scene, something that no one found.

I was pondering the Turkish visa requirements when I remembered my promise to Kiki. *After you read this, if there's nothing to find there, you let it go...*

I let out an audible growl and the guy next to me scurried down the train car. *Damn it, Kiki.*

I let my forehead rest against my hand. She was right. I had what I'd been looking for—the truth about Dad's death. It just wasn't the truth I'd expected. Instead, it was proof that there was nothing to find. Maybe it *was* time to start picking up the broken pieces of what life I had left, rather than diving deeper down the rabbit hole of conspiracy theories and wild suspicion.

I didn't relish the conversation I'd need to have with the med school dean.

I MADE it back to the apartment a little before noon.

Kiki emerged from her room, which we called the

"Keek-Cave," as it was piled high with computer monitors, external drives, and a million blinky lights I couldn't even begin to understand. "You okay?" she asked.

No. I nodded, though. "Sure."

"Nearly time for you to go get your purse. Want me to come with?"

I shook my head. I didn't think I could manage small talk, even with a best friend. I also really didn't feel like getting back on the subway. "Can I borrow your phone to call an Uber? I'll pay you back."

"Of course." She pulled her phone from her back pocket, handed it to me, and disappeared back into her cave.

I was halfway through calling my ride when a text popped up. I read it before I could help it. It was from a contact labeled as "K."

Vizol didn't want her involved.

The breath whooshed from my lungs. What the hell was this? Why was she talking about my dad with someone named K? I spun around so my back was to Kiki's doorway and quickly tapped the text to take me to the prior messages. I hastily remembered to raise my mental shields how Kiki had taught me, shielding my thoughts from her.

The text chain appeared on the screen. It was only four texts, all from the last few hours.

Kiki: I gave it to her.

K: Good.

Kiki: I feel bad. Doesn't she deserve the truth?
K: Vizol didn't want her involved.

My hands shaking, I quickly tapped on K's contact information and memorized the number. Then I closed out of the texts and called my Uber. I dropped Kiki's phone on her desk beside her. "All done. I'm going to wait downstairs."

She was already absorbed in her screens. "'K. Bye."

I hurried to the entryway table and wrote down the number on a slip of paper before I forgot it.

What the fuck was going on?

In the Uber I ran through the messages in my head, trying on different interpretations. Scenarios where Kiki hadn't just horribly betrayed me with some mystery person who'd known my dad. I kept coming back to one explanation. *"I gave it to her"* could only mean the report. *"Doesn't she deserve the truth?"* could only mean that the report Kiki had given me had been a fake. Or doctored somehow. Otherwise, she'd have been giving me the truth when she handed it over. And Vizol didn't want her involved... well, I didn't know what the hell that meant because Dad couldn't have been involved in the coverup of his own murder, could he have?

Adrenaline sang through my veins. I felt more alive and alert than I had in a long time.

Vindication tasted good.

I'd been right.

What I didn't know was what the hell I was going to do about it. Kiki wouldn't just admit that she'd lied and given me a fake report, right? I needed to find a way to catch her in her deception. Something more than the text messages.

The Uber driver, a young Ethiopian guy named Mehari, waited for me while I ran into the EMS station and retrieved my purse. I didn't get any particularly weird looks from the bored receptionist when she handed over my purse, which told me either she hadn't fished around in it, or she didn't know an illegal card duplicator when she saw one. Fine by me.

I pulled out the UN keycard with my face on it. I'd forgotten about it after Kiki had agreed to give me the report, but maybe it would come in handy after all. If I could get the real version of the report and prove that what Kiki had given me was fake, I'd have the evidence I needed to confront her and find out what had really happened to Dad.

Settled on a course of action, I relaxed back into the seat.

Until we got to the intersection just before my apartment, and I saw Kiki trotting down the stairs and into the back seat of a black car.

I surged forward between the front seats, pointing. "Follow that car!"

Mehari shot me an incredulous look. "This isn't a cab, lady. You have to book through the app."

I grumbled, fishing in my purse and pulling out some of Martin's cash. "I'll give you a hundred bucks if you follow that car. Off the record."

He blew out a sigh but took the money, sliding the car into gear. "You get half an hour, then you're out wherever we end up."

"I can live with that."

I WASN'T sure what type of clandestine meetup I'd been expecting, but a trip to the park was not it. We followed Kiki's car across the Queensboro bridge, circled back around, and took the small Roosevelt Bridge onto Roosevelt Island, a long narrow strip of land between Long Island and Manhattan. At the very tip of the island was a triangular park called Franklin D. Roosevelt Four Freedoms State Park (a mouthful, I know), which was where Kiki's car dropped her off.

Puzzled, and slightly irked that I'd just paid $100 bucks for a ten-minute ride, I hopped out and followed at a distance.

Kiki had never mentioned this park before. What was she doing here? Meeting someone? K, perhaps?

I'd never actually been to this park, either, despite living in New York most of my life. The tree-lined thoroughfare gave way to a stone monument at the tip of the island, and that was where Kiki was headed. I ogled the breathtaking skyline while trying to keep far enough back so she wouldn't see me.

Opening my glands wide, I took in her scent of coffee and coconut shampoo. It would be easier for me to track her at a distance this way.

I lingered behind the last tree before the open stone monument, as there was nowhere to hide from her if I continued. There were a few folks looking at the monument today, but they strolled back my way before too long. Kiki took a little set of steps leading down to the end of the island and stood there, looking out into the East River.

And then she disappeared.

I blinked twice. A third time. Flared my nostrils. But her smell was only a faint memory. She was gone.

What the fuck?

I jogged forward, no longer caring if she popped out from somewhere and caught me. Where had she gone?

My steps stilled at the spot where she'd disappeared. Her scent was stronger—she'd definitely been here. And she was definitely not here now. I peered over the edge into the water. Had she jumped? Gone for a swim? That made no sense. Kiki didn't even like hot tubs.

There was definitely something fishy going on here. Something I didn't understand, and Kiki was in on it. I turned on my heel and walked back towards the trees, settling down on the ground, my back to a hard trunk.

I was looking for answers. And there were answers here to be found. I could feel it. So I would wait.

In the meantime, I couldn't help but gaze at the United Nations tower, glittering like a shining jewel in the afternoon sun. It was directly across the channel from here. Could that be a coincidence?

I used to love coming to visit Dad at work when I was younger. The whole city was like some alien world, and within it, the MASC offices felt like home. Filled with supes of all shapes and sizes, Auntie warned me not to stare half a dozen times before she simply gave up.

I could just make out the statue in the center of the courtyard from here. It depicted the moment that everything had changed. The Lupine Offensive. When a pack of French wolf shifters had saved an Allied battalion pinned down by enemy fire. The day the world had learned that supernatural creatures existed.

After World War Two, in those brief shining months when the world had resolved to find a better way and had still been naive to all the conflicts to come, the United Nations Charter had been signed, together with the Treaty, officially recognizing supes.

MASC had been created as a division of the UN, and over the next decades, supes had started feeling safe to come out of the shadows. Wanting recognition and the benefits it brought—employment, security, access to financing and resources. There were currently six hundred and twelve recognized races of supernatural creatures. And that number grew every year. It wasn't a perfect system, but it was still miraculous as fuck. I knew I was lucky to live in a time where I could walk through New York City without hiding what I was.

My thoughts were interrupted as a figure appeared at the end of the island—right where Kiki had disappeared.

But it wasn't Kiki.

It was a man.

I breathed in deeply. He smelled like the space between—night air and the nothingness of fresh snow. This man was like a black hole for my senses. No heat signature. There, but not there. I took pride in my tolerance of the diversity of all forms of supernatural life, but I couldn't help the thought that darted through my mind, bright as a comet. *Unnatural.*

This man was a vampire.

5
———

I pretended to be fiddling with my phone as he stalked past where I sat, his gait graceful as a jungle cat.

It took every ounce of effort not to examine him as he walked by, to keep my eyes fixed on my phone. His beauty was breathtaking—sandy-blond hair pulled back in a tight knot at the nape of his neck, sky-blue eyes framed by slanting blond brows, an aquiline nose, square jaw, and dimple in his chin—just a few of the gifts he was graced with. He was well over six feet tall and built of lean, roping muscle, and though he was dressed in dark jeans, a white collared shirt, and a charcoal sports jacket, my animal senses had no problem identifying him for what he was.

Dangerous. Predator. My snake sense withdrew, even as my human side was fascinated. Drawn like a moth to a flame. Vampires had that effect on people.

Could this be the person Kiki was texting? Did this man know my dad somehow? I shoved to my feet, watching him as he walked away.

Only one way to find out.

I pulled the scrap of paper with the phone number out of my pocket and ducked behind the trunk of the closest tree. I turned my call blocking on and tapped in the number, biting my lip as it rang.

As I watched him break his stride and pull a cell phone out of his pocket.

Holy shit.

"Hello?" His voice was a deep baritone. "Who is this?"

I wiped my sweaty palms on my jeans, first one, then the other. Damn, this was more nerve-racking than prank calling our history teacher in fourth grade. "I'm looking for Kiki."

Pause. "Wrong number." He had a hint of an accent. I couldn't place it. I needed to keep him talking. To find out something more about him. He was still moving in the distance, and I started to follow. I could track him on scent alone, or rather, lack of scent, but I wanted to keep him in sight.

"I have a job I need done."

"What kind of job?"

I was freewheeling into space here. But I figured this guy fell into one of two categories. Either he was government, like Dad had been, or he was a bad guy.

I needed to know which. "I need...some intel from a high-level government target."

"Not exactly what we do."

"What is it you do then? I have a number of jobs I need completed, and I'm looking for...some special talent." I hardly recognized the bullshit coming out of my mouth, but I needed to get the guy talking. Anything. I needed a clue.

"We don't take third-party solicitation. Don't call this number again." The line went dead.

I frowned at my phone. His accent seemed European. German perhaps? Or Dutch?

Well, I hadn't learned much from the phone call, but I knew this was the right guy at least. Maybe he would lead me to my next clue.

I looked up and found him gone.

Damn it!

Shoving my phone in my back pocket, I trotted ahead, past a derelict stone building corralled behind a chain link fence. Where'd he gone?

I sniffed the air for his scent of starlight and black space. Emptiness, where the rest of the world was a tumble of smells. I smiled. *Gotcha.*

I jogged down the path after the mysterious Mr. K, my mind whirling to put the pieces together. I didn't have enough yet, that was about the only thing that was clear.

K was a vampire. He knew Kiki and my dad. He wasn't willing to access classified government data for me, which meant he could work for the government. Or he could just be a bad guy with a different skill set. I needed more—

A blur of golden darkness collided into me and my back hit the trunk of a tree hard enough to send a parade of stars dancing across my vision.

The vampire. He was attacking me!

Instinct kicked in and I spun and twisted out of his grip, thanking Dad for subjecting me to nearly two decades of mixed martial arts training. I ducked low and swiped my leg across the ground to knock him off his feet.

God, he was fast. He jumped and moved in close, grabbing one of my wrists.

But I was fast too. I flipped over him, freeing my wrist, and danced back, my pulse roaring in my ears.

The vampire was already coming at me again. He went for my wrists a second time, trying to restrain me. I darted back, but he was too fast.

His cold hand closed around my wrist like a shackle and when I went to spin—this time he was ready. He grabbed my other wrist and wrenched it up and over my head so both hands were pinned behind me, twisted at a painful angle. I kicked out at him but stumbled as he barreled me backwards against the truck of a tree, pinning me with his body —his powerful thighs pressing into and immobilizing my legs so I couldn't kick him.

I screamed with rage and struggled in his grip.

No one had bested me like this in a long fucking time. Certainly not in twenty seconds flat.

"Who are you?" He growled, pulling my wrists tighter, straining my shoulders in their sockets. "Why are you following me?"

I bared my teeth at him, showing my fangs.

He did the same—revealing straight white teeth and two wickedly pointed incisors. "I won't ask you again."

Something about the sight of those two fangs brought me back to myself, clearing the red clouding my vision. Leaving something small and frightened. Mortal. *Of course this supe bested you—you've been fighting for eighteen years.* He could have been fighting for hundreds. Thousands. There was no telling how old he was.

The vampire's nostrils flared, and I could feel his hard body relax slightly against mine. "That's better."

I hated that he could smell my fear. Stupid human hormones.

I glared at him. With my draining anger, my awareness returned to my body. To my predicament. To the man pressed up against the length of me.

This close, he was even more breathtaking—surrounding me, gazing down at me with fury in his eyes. There was a ring of silver around his irises, surrounded by the blue of a glacier. His pale skin was as flawless as marble. His breath was cool on my cheek; his scent this close carried a hint of mint leaves and musky cologne.

My body responded in another way, my fear mingling with something new. An undeniable warmth deep inside me. Desire. Suddenly, I was glad he was pinning me to the tree because I wasn't sure my knees would hold.

No. No, no, no—

My cheeks heated as his nostrils flared again and I knew he could smell my desire. His chest heaved where it was pressed against mine and his eyes dropped, lingering on my lips.

"It's common," he murmured. "Human physiology interacts with vampire pheromones in a predictable way."

My mortification doused any semblance of sexy-feelings.

"But you're naga," he said. "Not human." Dear lord, his eyes were still on my mouth.

"Half-naga." My words were breathy.

His eyes flicked up at that and he recoiled slightly. Coming back to himself. "If I step away, can we talk? You won't run?"

I nodded and he dropped his iron grip on my wrists, taking a big step back.

I sagged against the tree. With the heat of the moment gone, everything hurt. Rolling my shoulders, I rubbed my wrists. I'd have a bruise where a knot of tree bark had jammed into my back.

"Who are you?" he asked again.

"I think you already know," I hazarded a guess. The way he'd reacted to the fact that I was half-naga, and the fact that he knew my father...

"Zariya Chanji."

"In the flesh." I gave a little fake bow with a twirl of my hand. "Your turn."

"The name's Bauer."

"Uh-uh." I made a little buzzer noise. "Try again."

He let out an exasperated sigh. "Konstantin Bauer."

"How did you know my father?"

"We worked together. In the past. I know it may be hard to believe when we met like this, but I cared about your father. He was a good man. His death grieved me."

I scrutinized Konstantin, trying to get a read on him. I could generally detect lying in humans, as my glands picked up their increased heart rates, their raised body temperature. But Konstantin was a black hole of cool, his body giving nothing away.

Yet his face did appear sincere. His annoyingly perfect face.

"What really happened in Turkey?" I asked. "How did he die? I know that report Kiki gave me is bogus."

"It's not bogus," he said. "I did edit out a few confidential details. You have to understand that much of the work your father did was classified. He wouldn't want you involved. Knowledge can be dangerous."

"I don't care! I know Dad's death wasn't an accident. Someone killed him, and I have the right to know who. I *have* to know who. Don't you get it?" I hated the thickness in my voice. The tears that threatened to spill.

"I understand you're grieving—"

"You don't understand shit!" Oh god, the tears were coming now. My words wavered. "Nagas avenge our dead. It's my right. I won't be able to rest until I do. Dad won't be able to rest until I do."

His gaze hardened and certainty flooded me. This man knew something.

"Stop digging, Zariya. There's nothing to find."

I nodded, letting my shoulders slump. Pretending to be cowed.

He hesitated, and then stepped in, laid a gentle hand on my shoulder. "Be well, Zariya. Live your life. It's what Vizol would have wanted."

I tried to hide my shock as I caught sight of a mark on his palm—a mark I recognized. A brand that had graced my own father's hand. A circle, sliced diagonally by what appeared to be a cross.

This vampire had a matching one.

I stood silently as he walked away, disappearing around the bend.

And then I smiled. I'd gotten what I needed, and more besides.

Someone *had* killed my father. And this vampire knew who. Maybe he was protecting the killer, or maybe he wanted his own revenge, but either way, I'd find out whom the murderer was if it was the last thing I did.

6

———

Konstantin strode along the tree-lined path towards the other end of the park, where a wrought-iron fence separated it from the asphalt streets of Roosevelt Island. The base—"Tartarus," they called it—after one of the realms of the Greek underworld—sprawled beneath much of the island, five levels down at its deepest. You could access Tartarus through an emergency entrance near the UN building on the Manhattan side of the river, but the area was more heavily populated, so they were all commanded to use the island entrances unless absolutely necessary. It never ceased to amaze him that millions of New Yorkers could go about their lives ignorant of the secret military base right beneath their feet. But he supposed the set of highly-advanced magical safeguards protecting Tartarus from discovery had something to do with that.

Konstantin had been on the clock for over forty-eight hours, burning through intel to track down a group of supe-poaching assholes who called themselves "the Collectors." He'd been looking forward to heading home to enjoy the wagyu beef steak he had marinating, together with a glass of full-bodied red wine.

Zariya Chanji had thrown a wrench in those plans.

Vizol had spoken of his daughter often and with pride. Konstantin had heard about her growing up, winning Krav Maga competitions against kids twice her age. He'd bragged when she'd gone to Columbia, pre-med, and when she'd gotten into Cornell's medical school, which had one of the nation's leading supe medicine programs.

In his mind, Zariya had still been the gangly kid smiling out of the photos on Vizol's desk.

He hadn't been prepared for the reality of her in the flesh.

She was tall and lithe, with all the sinuous curves of her naga heritage. Her glossy black hair pulled into a thick braid, her smooth caramel skin unmarred but for two streaks of golden scales running up her neck to her temples. She was the picture of an Indian beauty —full lips, delicate cheekbones, thick black eyelashes framing arresting green eyes. Slitted, snake eyes. She'd moved with the same kind of sinuous grace Vizol had, though her moves were perhaps a bit rusty.

She'd been fierce and beautiful, and clearly falling apart over her father.

In his six hundred years, he'd lost more people than he could count. He'd seen war and hardship and the worst of human cruelty. He'd developed a thick skin—he'd had to. So he hadn't been prepared for just how much Zariya's furious grief would move him.

Konstantin stepped into the doorway of the vacant building, flashing his ring at the scanner. The portal's magic picked up the signature of his ring and whisked him down into the elevator bay. He pressed the button for the third floor.

The doors opened to reveal a utilitarian gray hallway. The base had been costly enough to build, so there hadn't been a lot left over in the budget to fancy it up.

He strode down the hallway, hanging a left into the Operations Center, a broad room filled with monitors and computers. Kiki, their technical wizard and resident hacker, was working at one bank of monitors, her noise-canceling headphones shutting out the world. Konstantin knew those headphones dulled more than noise; they were magicked to quiet the mental projections of those in the base, letting Kiki work without having to keep firm mental walls up at all times.

Konstantin tapped her on the shoulder, and she turned, pulling them down around her neck. "Thought you were heading home."

"I came back after I had an unexpected meeting in the park." Konstantin let down his own mental shields, letting Kiki see what had happened.

Her dark eyes went wide and she clapped a hand over her mouth. "Ohmygod, Konstantin, I'm so sorry. How..." She trailed off. "She had my phone. To call an Uber. It must have been when you texted... Damn it!" She slouched on the desk for a moment, her head in her hands.

Konstantin waited.

Kiki pushed herself back up. "What are you going to do? Maybe we should just tell her. This whole thing has me feeling like shit."

"You know the rules," Konstantin said, though he saw her point.

"Rules are made to be broken." Kiki waggled her pierced eyebrows. "Maybe she could help us with the investigation. Help us see something we haven't. She knew Vizol better than anyone."

Konstantin shook his head. "We need to respect her father's wishes. He didn't want her to know about this place. What we do here. I'm sure that would extend to investigating his own murder."

"But that was back when she was all happy and

going to be a doctor. Now she's washed out and miserable and...I think she needs this, K."

"No daughter needs to know that her father was lying to her for half her life. I doubt that would help the grieving process," he said. Kiki started to open her mouth to object and he held up a hand. "Besides. It's not my call. The Director has to decide whether anyone's brought into the fold. I'm going to talk to him now. I'll let you know what he decides. Just wanted to give you a heads-up in case Zariya contacts you."

Kiki pouted. "Roger that, boss."

Konstantin headed down the hallway towards the Director's office. He passed a set of wide windows that looked into the gym and sparring room. The valkyrie Alviya was sparring with Strongroot, a sequoia dryad and her team leader. He towered over her, but she was fiercely maneuverable and darted around him like a hornet.

Konstantin frowned. He knew Alviya lived with Kiki and Zariya—marking yet another person in Zariya's life who was lying to her. He wasn't so sure that Kiki was right. Instead of giving the woman something to live for, revealing the truth of their operation to her might just be the thing that would break her.

Konstantin knocked on the thick door at the end of the hallway.

"Come in," came the muffled reply.

Konstantin found Cyriaque Broussard sitting behind his desk, a pair of reading glasses perched on his nose. He looked out of place, his slacks and blue button-down incongruous against his thick beard and wild shock of dark curls. Like he'd been domesticated.

"Konstantin," the werewolf said, motioning to the chair in front of his desk. "Thought you headed home."

"Was going to. But we've got a bit of a problem." Konstantin quickly brought Director Broussard up to speed.

Broussard took off his glasses and pinched the bridge of his nose. "That girl always was too inquisitive for her own good. I remember at one of her birthday parties—maybe she was nine? She rifled around her aunt's purse and swiped a scrying crystal so she could see through the wrapping of all her presents." He chuckled. "Vizol could barely keep a straight face while he was scolding her."

Konstantin sank into the chair. "I guess I didn't realize you were so close with the family."

"Well, Vizol didn't like to talk about it, make anyone else feel uncomfortable or like I got special treatment. But I think I was one of the first friendly faces he met when he moved to the States. I convinced him to join the Marines."

Konstantin nodded woodenly. Yet another person in Zariya's life whom wasn't who she thought he was.

"I wish he were still here. Then he'd be sitting behind this desk instead of me. If I'd known how much goddamn paperwork came with this job..." He growled. "Don't let them put you behind this desk someday when I'm gone."

"You've only had the job for six weeks. You're going to be sitting in that chair for a good long while, sir," Konstantin said. "Now, what would you like to do about Zariya? I've spoken to Kimiko, and she expressed an interest in bringing Zariya in. She had the interesting thought that she might be able to help us with our investigation—"

"That's a non-starter, Konstantin," Broussard said. "You know that."

He sighed. "Wasn't sure it was a good idea myself. I just thought it was worth mentioning."

"We've got better resources than every government in the world put together. We'll find the bastards who took down Vizol."

"Yes, sir."

"But Zariya is bound to keep digging. If she's anything like her father—and she is—she'll be a dog with a bone. We have to wipe the slate clean."

He frowned. "Wipe the—wipe her memory? But that can be dangerous—"

"Verte's been working on a way to make it more targeted. It won't take more than a few days of her memory. She'll be fine."

"I don't like it."

"Neither do I. I'm telling you, it's shit sitting behind this desk. But it's what needs to be done."

Konstantin ran his tongue over the tips of his fangs. It didn't sit well with him, but Broussard was right. "Fine. I'll get the potion from Verte. I'll administer it myself."

Broussard waved a hand. "Don't Alviya and Kimiko live with her? Have one of them do it. It'll be easy for them to slip the potion to her."

"Don't you think that's a little...personal? Asking them to wipe their friend's memory?"

"No one ever said this job was easy, Bauer. They can draw straws, but one of those two is dosing Zariya Chanji, and it happens tonight."

Konstantin stood. "Consider it done."

"Close the door on the way out," Broussard said, and Konstantin obliged, thinking all the while that Cyriaque Broussard was turning out to be a very different director than Vizol Chanji had been.

7

I sank to the ground under the tree where Konstantin had left me. I decided to stay here until I was sure my wobbly legs would cooperate.

A maelstrom of emotions threatened to overwhelm me. Anger. Fear. Desire. Resolve. They warred within me, leaving me sucking in deep breaths to ground myself. As overwhelming as it all was, after six weeks of nothing but numbness, it felt good to feel alive again.

My phone rang. I startled and let out a little squeal of surprise before pulling it from my back pocket.

It was my Aunt Temsula, Dad's sister. She'd called me every day since Dad had died, though I had gone for weeks without picking up. Finally, she'd stormed into the apartment for an intervention when it had gone on too long—bringing incense to dispel the bad spirits and homemade lamb curry to fill my belly. I'd started taking her calls after that.

"Hi, Auntie," I answered.

"Hello, my little curlicue," she replied, using the pet name she'd used since I'd been a girl. Snake joke. "You sound good today."

"I'm out," I admitted.

"Praise Manasa," Auntie trilled into the phone. "Tell me about your day."

Not likely. I cleared my throat, leaning my head back against the tree. "I ran some errands. Went to the park with Kiki." That was sort of true, right?

"Oh, Zariya, I am so pleased. I know you grieve, but it is a beautiful world. Life has so much in store for you." Auntie hadn't really raised me, but close enough. Every time Dad had been traveling for work, which was a lot, I'd stay with her. She believed that over-mothering and over-dramatics were her auntie birthright.

I swallowed. Auntie's unbridled optimism always made me want to cry. Sometimes I wished I could see the world the way she did. "Do you remember that mark on Dad's hand? The brand?"

She was quiet for a moment. "Yes. Why do you ask?"

"Tell me again how he got it?" I wanted to hear her version, to see if it matched my own memory. I remembered being cuddled up next to Dad on the couch while he'd read to me from *Grimm's Fairy Tales*. He'd always read the gruesome, old-timey versions of the stories, not the pretty, glossed-over Disney versions. My cheek was pressed against his bare chest, and I'd kept asking about his scars. Those were the stories I wanted to hear—our stories—not some stories from a world I barely recognized.

"Our clan consisted of renowned warriors around the continent," he'd said. "But before we were allowed to become full warriors, we were required to perform a feat of great bravery. To prove our worthiness. I was young and foolish and was determined to perform the most memorable feat in the history of our clan. There was a rumor of a dragon deep in the mountains, who protected the burial site of the great Naga King Vasuki. The tomb was supposedly filled with treasure. I knew if I brought back a piece of that treasure and bested the dragon that my name would go down in history. I found the tomb, but it fought me, even before I found the dragon. It was rigged with booby traps and terrible magics."

"Like Indiana Jones," I'd said. Those were some of my favorite movies.

"Exactly. But I found my way to the center—the tomb of the ancient king himself. But the dragon was not just a legend. He was there, in the flesh, and he was strong. I was in over my head, and before long, eager flames licked up around me, and I knew I needed to slay the beast if I had any hope of escaping with my life. So I seized a sword from the great king's treasure trove and plunged it into the creature's chest."

"But the sword was burning hot from the fire, and a symbol from the scabbard branded you," I'd finished for him. It wasn't the first time I'd heard the story.

"Exactly. I wear this brand with honor. It reminds me of that brave beast, which laid down its life guarding that which it had been charged to protect."

"A bunch of stuff?" I'd wrinkled my nose. "Did you at least keep the sword?"

"As the dragon fell, the temple began to collapse. I knew that I had meddled with something great, something beyond my understanding. I left the sword, taking only my brand as proof of my worthiness. Some things are best left undiscovered, hatchling. Some magics are too much for the world."

Auntie's answer interrupted my memory. "He got it battling that dragon."

"Do you remember when he went for his quest?"

Another pause. "Yes, but I don't see why this—"

"And he said he lost the sword, right? That it was destroyed."

"Yes. He brought nothing back but that mark on his hand. Why do you ask?"

I chewed my lip. "No reason. I was just thinking

about Dad's stories. Wondering how many of them were really true."

"They were all true, my darling. Your father was a great warrior. And a great naga."

"Thanks," I said. "I need to go, Auntie. Talk to you tomorrow?"

"Tomorrow, curlicue. I love you. And eat something!"

I rolled my eyes. "Love you too."

I hung up the phone and stared at it.

It didn't add up. The story—the identical brand on Konstantin's palm. How could a European vampire have been branded by a lost sword deep in the Indian jungle? I couldn't escape the unwelcome conclusion. Either Dad had been lying to me, or Auntie was.

I didn't know which was worse.

I WALKED off Roosevelt Island to dispel my nervous energy, but it still pinged about my veins like fireflies in a bottle. I wasn't ready to go home yet, to face Kiki when she returned.

Would Konstantin tell her I'd followed him? Would she say something? Or would she say nothing at all, pretending like there wasn't a huge fat lie between us?

An hour later, I found myself at the sparring gym,

a large brick building where Dad and I had spent many nights. Even though I hadn't grown up among our clan, Dad had said all nagas were warriors and needed to learn to fight.

I'd loved those times when it had been just the two of us, Dad gently correcting my footing or the angles of my strikes. Even when he'd worked me until I'd wanted to vomit, I'd relished every minute with him. Here, I'd never felt like I was trapped between worlds. Here, we were nagas.

"Chanji!" the owner, Sal, a shaggy-haired cougar shifter, jogged over and wrapped me in a hug.

He rocked me back and forth, and I let myself relax against his muscled form. Sal had been like an uncle to me, overseeing my training when Dad had been traveling or working. "We've missed you around here, Cobra Kai." Another nickname. Another snake joke.

I pulled back, hastily wiping a tear that had gathered on my lashes. "I just...I haven't been getting out much."

He wrapped an arm around me and walked me towards one of the sparring rings. "Moving the body is good for the soul, Zariya. Emotions get stored in the body—stagnate there. I think coming back here more regularly could help, in its own small way."

Everyone had their advice, and I found most of it unwelcome. But Sal's carried a simplicity that resonated with me.

He continued. "But what do I know? I'm just a shaggy old cat a bit too long in the tooth."

"Hardly." I smiled wistfully. Sal was still muscled like a young Arnold Schwarzenegger, with neat sandy hair and a trim beard. "You're probably right. Sleeping my life away certainly hasn't helped much."

"What do you want to work on today?" he asked, all business. I appreciated that about Sal. Here, it was simple.

"Actually, I came across a vamp today who pulled some moves on me I couldn't get out of."

Sal's gold eyes flashed, and I could swear I could see his hackles rising. "What are you crossing vamps for?"

"It was a...misunderstanding. But do you think you could work with me on finding a way around his moves?"

Sal grinned, stepping into the ring. "With pleasure, Cobra Kai."

8

———

My mind was clearer than it had been in a long while when I headed home from the gym. I'd forgotten how good a hard workout felt—how it turned off my thoughts and filled me with endorphins. Sal had made me promise I'd return later that week, and I'd been happy to agree. I felt more like myself than I had since Dad had died.

I stopped at my favorite bodega for some falafel as I strolled home. I actually liked to cook—Auntie was a miracle worker in the kitchen and I'd always worked as her sous chef when Dad had been traveling. But our fridge was currently an empty black hole and my stomach was demanding something quick.

I sat at one of the little rickety tables on the street, pondering how the hell I would get into Kiki and Konstantin's hidden lair. I still didn't understand the connection between them or how they appeared and disappeared in the middle of a city park, but magic was obviously involved.

I closed my eyes for a moment at the thought of Konstantin Bauer, my mouth going dry, and not just from the falafel. I hadn't dated much in college, too focused on school and my studies, and med school had been even worse. There had been a fling or two, and a few ill-advised one-night stands, but the pickings had always been slim, as humans were off-limits. I hadn't been prepared for how my body had responded to his nearness.

Vampires had always been the celebrities of the supe world, and there were vampire groupies that got off on drawing a vamp's eye. It certainly didn't hurt that a few drops of vampire blood were all it took to turn a human into a glassy-eyed thrall who would do whatever the vamp told them. That was why the substance was strictly, aggressively banned.

But I'd never considered myself into vampires. If anything, I'd avoided them. They were ancient, dangerous, arrogant, unpredictable. Though somehow, when applied to Konstantin Bauer, all of those adjectives became downright delectable.

I shook my head, realizing I'd drifted into a dreamy fog, my fingertips lingering on my lips. "Cool it, Zariya," I muttered to myself, devouring another bite of falafel. He was the enemy. I didn't care if he'd known my dad and knew Kiki now. He was resolved to keep information from me that I needed. That made him my adversary.

I finished my pita and headed back towards the apartment. I wasn't sure what to do about Kiki. How I'd go about finding the key to whatever mysterious other realm Kiki had disappeared into. Maybe my glands would be able to smell something that would clue me in to the key.

But I wasn't prepared for what I found when I got home.

Alviya and Bas were posted up on the couch, watching Netflix and munching on a bowl full of popcorn.

"Hey, Zar." Alviya perked up as I came through the door. "Where've you been today?"

When a person doesn't leave their room for six weeks, I supposed that any trip out of the house was cause for celebration.

I sank onto the couch on Alviya's other side. "Went for a walk, then I went to the dojo and sparred with Sal for a while."

"That's great!" Bas said, baring his straight white teeth in a grin. "We should all work out together some time."

"That would be fun," I said halfheartedly, knowing that Alviya and Bas were in way better shape than I was.

"Popcorn?" Alviya offered me the bowl.

And I froze.

My glands flared.

I recognized the smell coming off Alviya. It was faint but undeniable. Starlight and empty space. Ice and deep water and stagnant snow. The smell of Konstantin Bauer.

I took a handful of popcorn to cover my shock. Alviya knew Konstantin. Or had at least met him. Encountered him. "How was work today?" I managed.

Alviya shrugged. "Business as usual. Office stuff. Boring."

"You meet any new clients, or have meetings out of the office?" Inwardly, I cringed at my inelegant questions.

"Naw." Alviya didn't seem to notice. "Just chained to my desk, as per usual."

I nodded, piling popcorn into my mouth. I had no idea how to fit this new piece into the puzzle. I was getting closer to something—but what—I had no idea.

Alviya, Bas, and I powered through two episodes of *Fixer Upper* before I headed off to bed. Kiki still wasn't home, which was okay by me. I needed to make my move quickly and try to find the real version of the report. I could keep my mental shields up for a while, but I wasn't great about mental discipline. If I let it go more than a few days without talking to her, she'd probably pick up my thoughts without even trying.

I had to confront her. It was the only way to get to the bottom of things. Kiki and I had been friends for too long to leave such a huge gulf between us. Besides, judging by the text to Konstantin, she'd felt bad about giving me a report that didn't have all the details. Maybe I could guilt her into telling me the truth.

After I made my mind up about how I'd handle Kiki, I finally fell into a deep sleep.

I woke to a prickle in my awareness.

Someone was in my room.

Moving only infinitesimally, I opened my glands. Not only did naga glands grant us an incredible sense of smell, but they worked as infrared sensors. I could smell the heat in the room, conceptualize the size, dimensions. It was a small body—familiar. Kiki.

What was she doing?

Curious, I kept my breathing still and deep. My eyes closed.

She crept closer, and I felt as she stood over me. Watching me.

Her heartrate was elevating, her heat increasing.

Something was wrong.

"I'm so sorry," she whispered.

I caught her hand before she struck and rolled her onto the bed, pinning her.

She didn't struggle against me, even when I caught sight of the syringe in her hand.

"What the hell are you doing, Kiki?"

She started to cry.

I plucked the syringe from her fingers and sat up slightly so I wasn't holding her down. "What is this?"

She curled into a ball. "I'm so sorry, Zariya. It's to make you forget. It wouldn't hurt you. The place I work, it's top secret. They know you'd just keep digging."

"Konstantin," I said. "The vamp. Do you work for him?" I looked at the syringe in disbelief. He'd actually erase my memory? So I forgot our conversation, forgot how close I was getting to finding the truth about Dad's death? Anger flared to life in me, bright and hot.

"Not him, not exactly. I can't—I can't say," Kiki said.

"We've been friends for over ten years, Kiki, and you've been lying to me this whole time?"

"Not the whole time, Zariya, I swear. I never lied about the stuff that mattered."

"Like who killed Dad?" I scoffed. "I'm going to find out. You can't stop me."

Kiki's eyes flashed and she sat up. She snatched for the syringe, but I was too fast and moved it out of her range.

Her mind flashed out, her thoughts barreling through my pitiful defenses. She was inside my mind, raining her will down upon me like a hailstorm. Kiki wasn't much of a physical fighter, but with her mind—she was deadly.

But I was ready. I lunged and stabbed her in the thigh with the syringe, emptying the vial with one quick shove of my thumb.

Her mental barrage stilled in shock.

"How do I get into the facility?" I asked her. I didn't have her satori gifts, but her mind was inside mine, her thoughts frozen in surprise. It was enough. A mental image flashed by and I caught it. She made an involuntary fist, curling her hand into her stomach.

Bingo. Kiki's ring was my ticket through the portal in the park.

She slumped back against the bed as the memory potion in the syringe went to work. I pulled a silver ring etched with a pattern of bamboo leaves from her middle finger and slipped it onto my own.

I stood, staring at her passed-out body slumped on my bed. A flurry of mixed emotions buffeted me.

"I'm so sorry too, Kiki," I said softly. I *was* sorry it had come to this. That she had pushed us to this. But I wasn't sorry for taking her ring. Because it was time to get the answers I deserved.

9

___

My guilt over leaving Kiki passed out in my bed, next to an empty syringe, was short-lived. *She was going to use it on me first!* Still, I prayed there weren't any negative side effects. If this ring didn't get my answers, Kiki was my best hope of figuring out what the hell was actually going on.

The ride to Roosevelt Island felt endless. When the Uber driver dropped me off at the entrance to the park, I practically launched myself from the car, jogging towards the island's apex. The city skyline was breathtaking from here—noble towers shimmering with endless lights.

I'd dressed in black jeans, an old gray tee, and my green army-style jacket. I'd threaded the sheath for the knife Dad had given me for my sixteenth birthday through my belt, but I really, really hoped I didn't need to use it. My muscles were already sore from my workout with Sal, and if my run-in with Konstantin had shown me anything, it was that these guys were good—whoever they might be.

The park was deserted except for a couple nestled under a tree, far too wrapped up in each other to notice me. My steps slowed when I neared the point where Kiki had disappeared. Would I know how to summon the magic that had whisked her away? Suddenly, I wished I'd asked her more or had tried to rifle around in her thoughts when they'd been exposed to me. Maybe there was a magic password that I was missing and I'd just stand here in the cold, like an idiot.

I stepped forward. "Come on, come on—"

My stomach dropped out from under me as the world spun, shifting into something new.

"Yes!" I exclaimed with a pump of my fist. No magic password or spell. Then I flinched, realizing that my voice was now echoing throughout an enclosed space.

I looked around. I was alone in a gray concrete alcove, surrounded by walls on three sides. And before me, an elevator door.

"Looks like I'm going down," I whispered, pressing the button.

The door opened and I stepped in, turning to examine my options. Buttons for floors one through five stared mutely at me. I bit my lip. Which floor had the answers I sought? And more importantly, which floor opened to a nice empty hallway, rather than a mess hall full of soldiers?

I opened my glands and quested below me, seeing if I could sense bodies. There was nothing but cold stone and rock. Either there was no one home, or whatever materials they'd used to build this place blocked my naga senses. I suspected the latter.

On instinct, I pressed the button for the fifth floor. Might as well go all the way.

My heart seemed to race down before I did as the elevator started to move. Had my dad ever ridden in this elevator? Konstantin had clearly known my father, but in what capacity?

The elevator stopped moving and my hand gravitated to the knife at my hip. Not that it would be much use against automatic weapons.

The doors opened to an empty hallway and I nearly sagged with relief. A shaky laugh escaped me. I prayed my luck would hold.

Now that I was down in the bowels of the place, my glands could sense all the spaces of this floor. There were two people on floor five—in rooms lining the hallway. I'd skip those in my investigation.

I started forward, unsure what the hell I was looking for. Anything. Answers. I poked my head through a doorway and found a quiet room lined with filing cabinets. I perked up. Files were good. Files had answers.

The cabinets were arranged alphabetically, and so I opened up the drawer containing the C files. Chanji seemed a good place to start.

I thumbed through the files and my breath caught. There he was. Vizol Chanji. I pulled the file from the drawer and scanned it, my slitted pupils helping me in the low light. *MASC Veil Force Personnel File*, the title read. In the upper left-hand corner was a symbol—a circle bisected by a diagonal cross. A symbol I recognized as the one that had marked both my dad's palm and Konstantin's. It couldn't be a coincidence. "Veil Force?" I puzzled out loud. "What the hell is that?" My father had worked for MASC, the Mythical Alliance of Supernatural Creatures, as a diplomat. How could he work for this—Veil Force—also?

But it was undeniably my dad's much younger face gazing out of the photo. His roles were listed below.

2001-2011-Hydra Team Commander

2011-2020-Director

I sat my ass down in a chair before my knees gave out. According to this file, Dad hadn't just been involved in this organization, he'd been the fucking head of it. Not to mention he'd been involved in it for nearly my entire life—meaning he'd been lying to me for basically as long as I could talk.

A tear trickled down my cheek. It had always been me and him. I'd thought we'd told each other everything. How could he have kept something like this from me? Why?

My glands sensed movement in the hallway and I froze. Someone was coming. Maybe they'd just pass by this room, headed farther down the hallway. *Come on, come on—*

The light flicked on.

Shit.

I don't think he saw me right away. The incredibly handsome man in a white doctor's lab coat. He had strawberry blond hair, exotic golden eyes tilted up at the corner, and bronze skin that seemed out of place beneath the sad fluorescent lights flicking to life above us. He was tall and well-built and formed far too perfect a picture to be human. This man was a supe.

He blinked when he saw me and halted mid-step, a file in his hand.

It was the only opening I'd get.

I bolted from the chair and barreled past him into the hallway.

"Hey!" he shouted after me.

But I was already booking it towards the elevator, moving at a breakneck pace.

"Lock down the elevator," he said to whoever was at the other end of his comm. "We've got an intruder on the fifth floor." He had an Australian accent, I noticed, as I slammed into the open elevator and jammed the button for the ground floor. Maybe I'd get lucky and start moving before they managed to lock it down.

The button lit up and the doors started to close. I grinned victoriously.

Then the doors stopped.

My luck had run out.

"Stay there." He advanced on me, arms out in front of him. Why, so he could jab a needle in my neck like Kiki had planned to? Fuck that.

I darted out of the elevator and ran straight towards him with a naga war cry, my fangs bared.

I didn't know what my plan was. I had no plan. Knock him over and barricade myself in one of the file rooms before going down in a blaze of glory?

I was stuck inside a secret base and there was no way they'd let me out voluntarily. But at least I could go down fighting.

The air seemed to shimmer and shift around the doctor. I gasped as every hair on my skin raised. It was the feeling in the air right before a lightning strike. Or right before a shifter changed form.

Hot Aussie doctor was a shifter.

I zigzagged against the wall, trying to make space for whatever was about to manifest in this hallway.

And boy was I glad I did.

Magic exploded around me as he finished shifting. And then the hallway was filled with legs and talons and a sleek sinuous body covered in golden scales.

Holy fuck. A dragon shifter. He was a fucking dragon.

His roar rent the air and I clapped my hands over my ears, staggering to one knee. My fingers came away bloody as I scrambled to my feet and hurtled myself down the hallway, towards any sort of protection from the dragon.

He was big—too big to maneuver in the hallway, and I looked over my shoulder to see him struggling to turn around—his massive body smashing against the walls, cracking the concrete.

I wrenched open an iron door at the end of the hallway, slamming it shut behind me.

I looked about in a mad panic for anything I could use to defend myself. The knife on my belt was nothing more than a toothpick to a dragon. The room was some sort of treasure room—with art in glass cases on two walls, the other two covered with glass cabinets bearing ancient-looking antiquities. Weapons.

A sword. Prominently placed in one cabinet on the far wall was an ornate sword. That might be enough.

I yanked at the cabinet door, but it was locked. I smashed it with my elbow—once, twice.

The room's iron door exploded inward and I was thrown against the cabinet, my hands scrabbling against the broken glass.

The dragon shoved its head through the door

and screamed, baring glistening white fangs as long as my forearm.

Pain exploded in my ears and my heart seized with fear, my limbs freezing, my mind numb. It didn't matter that the dragon was too big to get in the door. Dragons breathed fire. One shot and I was toast. Charred toast.

The sword.

My naga instincts screamed at me, singing life into my veins and overpowering the paralysis of my human fear. I wouldn't go down without a fight. I would show this pretender the true might of the serpent.

I reached into the case and seized the sword's scabbard, pulling it from its hooks.

And then the sword in my hand started to burn.

I screamed as pain ripped through my hand and up my arm. The sword was magicked somehow—it must have been a protective enchantment. The sword clattered to the floor as I cradled my injured hand against me. I looked down at the burn and gasped.

The same symbol was burned into my palm as had been branded into my father's. And Konstantin's. I looked at the sword with new realization dawning. Somehow, this blade was the same sword from my father's story. He'd always said he'd left it in the dragon's lair. Another lie.

An explosion across the room startled me back to where I was. The dragon had broken through the wall, busting the concrete around the door frame to create a hole large enough for his body to get through. He advanced on me now, his fangs bared, his golden eyes ablaze with fury.

The fight drained out of me. I was trapped. This creature could snap me in one bite. Even if I somehow got past him, I would never get up the elevator and get free. Was Dad's secret worth dying for?

I held up my hands, the burn throbbing on one palm. "I surrender."

The dragon hissed at me, and then its eyes went wide. Its head snaked close, examining the burn, sniffing at me with huge nostrils. I knew he was intelligent, that there was a man in there, but still my stomach quaked with fear at his nearness.

The clamor of boots reached my ears and I turned to the gaping doorway just in time for Konstantin to appear, half a dozen armed men behind him.

"You." His weapon was trained on me. The dragon's body was still between us, but it vanished in an instant as the shifter returned to human form.

"She's surrendered," the shifter said as Konstantin approached in one fluid movement, the muzzle of his gun still fixed upon me.

And then he shot me.

THE CHANJI GIRL crumpled to the ground before him.

"God damn it, Konstantin! She surrendered." Oliver knelt down to feel her pulse. "You didn't need to shoot her."

"Quit your bitching. It was a tranq dart," Konstantin bit back. "I didn't need her making a last desperate try for freedom. You could've brought the whole fucking base down. Look at this place." Konstantin surveyed the lower level in dismay. The entire length of the hallway would need reinforcing, the framing and drywall into the Antiquities locker would need replacing—Broussard would be pissed as hell. While they had fairly generous funding thanks to some creative earmarking in the MASC budget, they all preferred using those funds on cutting edge technologies and research, rather than cleaning up their base. "What were you thinking?" he hissed at the doctor. "And will you put on some pants?"

Oliver straightened, standing proudly as naked as the day he'd been born. "I was thinking we had an intruder in our most sensitive level and I needed to do anything necessary to stop her."

"And you needed to shift to do that? You couldn't have used some of that Special Forces training?"

"She's a supe! A naga!" Oliver protested.

"She's only half-naga."

Broussard stepped into the room behind them,

his thick arms crossed before him. If he was put out by the destruction, he wasn't showing it. "She's the daughter of Vizol Chanji and not to be underestimated. Get her to the medical bay and I want her restrained when she wakes. Oliver, put some fucking pants on. Bauer, with me."

"It marked her," Oliver called as Broussard turned to go.

"What?" The Director paused.

"*Caledfwlch*. The sword. She picked it up to defend herself and it marked her. She's been chosen."

Broussard nodded stiffly. "We'll deal with it."

Konstantin bit back a curse. This was a bigger clusterfuck than Gallipoli.

Konstantin fell into step next to the Director, who asked, "How did this happen? I thought we were settled in our course of action."

"We were." Konstantin ground his teeth. "Kimiko went home with the memory serum. I can only assume something went wrong there."

"Have we spoken to Nakamura?"

"You know as much as I do."

Broussard stormed into his office, bracing himself against the shelves. When he turned, his eyes were flashing, his fangs lengthened.

Konstantin held his ground. Vampires and werewolves had been historic enemies, but Konstantin had fought alongside many shifters in his day, especially the Rougarou—the Cajun wolves like Broussard. He respected the man and the position of leadership he was in, but Konstantin was an equal in power and skill. He wouldn't be intimidated.

Broussard sank into his chair, his head in his hands. "Vizol wouldn't have let something like this happen."

"We don't know that."

"Tartarus has never been breached."

Konstantin leaned down, his hands braced on the back of one of the chairs opposite Broussard. "With due respect, sir, I'm less concerned for how it happened and more worried about where we go from here.

That seemed to shake the Director back to himself. "Fair point. Send a Phantom to find out what happened to Kimiko. Let's get Alviya here too; they're friends, right? Perhaps it will calm Chanji to see a familiar face when she wakes." Konstantin wasn't sure knowing another friend had been lying to her would calm Zariya, but he swallowed the comment.

"What about the brand?" He found himself inadvertently fingering the mark on his own palm and stilled his hands.

"You know what it means, Konstantin. She's one of us. The sword chooses who is worthy."

"But we only let it test those who've trained. Who have fought. Our Phantoms are ex-Special Forces, ex-

CIA—the mostly highly trained fighters, intelligence officers, and assassins from around the globe. We can't just let her in because the sword picked her. It was a fluke. She never should have been near enough to touch it."

"Wasn't King Arthur chosen by the sword when he was just a boy?"

"That's just in the Disney version," Konstantin said. "Caledfwlch was gifted to him by the fae to mark his sovereignty over Britain—marked him as protector and lord of the land. Just as it marked Vizol as protector of the supernatural races. As it has marked each of us."

"Including Zariya—"

"I'm not saying she shouldn't be a Phantom eventually if she wants to. I'm not denying that she has potential. But she would need to train. We only recruit those who are already fully capable, who've worked in the field for years. We should wait—"

"You don't have time to wait." A female voice sounded from the doorway.

Konstantin turned to find Signe Dirksen striding into the room. Signe was a norn, a Scandinavian fae with the power to see the threads of fate. And sometimes change them. Signe's knowledge of magic was incredible, just as her sister, Verte's, grasp of science and technology were beyond anything Konstantin could even hope to understand. The two of them both worked from the base at Tartarus but were integral to the success of Veil Force as a whole, and the teams' missions in the field.

"What have you seen?" Cyriaque leaned forward.

"Just snatches of futures," Signe said. "They started when Zariya breached the base. But enough to know that in each of them, Zariya is key to Veil Force's future. Perhaps all of our futures." She turned to Konstantin. "Yours especially."

Konstantin crossed his arms before him. He didn't see how one willful half-human could have any influence on his future, even if she was Vizol's daughter.

"So that's it," Cyriaque said. "She's in."

"No." Signe was still looking at Konstantin with those penetrating blue eyes. Though Signe was physically blind, it didn't stop her from seeing more than the rest of them put together. Her magic more than made up for any lack of physical ability. "Konstantin is right. If we ignore the rules with Zariya, it will undermine the Phantoms' confidence in her. We need to be united as one."

"But you said we can't wait," Cyriaque pointed out. "What are you suggesting?"

"A test," Signe said. "Make Zariya pass a test to show she's worthy of joining. It's the only way to prove to all of us, and herself, that she belongs here."

"Sounds like a circus," Konstantin protested. "We don't have time for this. There's intel that the Collectors are moving again shortly—"

"We make time." Cyriaque stood. "We have to. You heard Signe. When has she ever led us astray?"

Konstantin sighed.

Cyriaque nodded to himself, resolved. "We will have this test. I'll oversee it myself."

11

I came to in a rush. The dragon shifter...the sword. It had burned me. I pulled my hand up to examine my palm and found myself restrained. Handcuffed to a bed.

What the hell?

I rattled the handcuffs, pulling at them. I was in some sort of laboratory. Machines blinked around me, and two other beds sat empty beside mine.

"Hey!" I called. "Let me go!"

The dragon shifter appeared around the corner, striding into the room and pulling up a stool beside me. I tried to inch away from him, but I was held fast. He didn't look angry, though—his tanned face was pleasant. "Zariya, I'm Dr. Oliver Connell. I think we got off on the wrong foot."

"How do you know who I am?" I asked. Had Kiki told him? Konstantin?

"You're well known to our organization. Through your father," Oliver said. "I'm sorry for your loss."

"Thanks," I said grudgingly.

"There's someone here to see you. Do you think you're up for visitors?"

My curiosity overcame my wariness. "Sure." My eyes widened when Alviya appeared around the corner, her red hair twisted in a braid over one shoulder.

"Hey." She sat down on the bed by my knees. "How are you feeling?"

"Like I got attacked by a dragon and shot with a tranq dart," I snapped. "What the hell are you doing here?"

She patted my leg and cleared her throat. "I work here, Zariya. I have for the last two years."

What the hell? "You work for a PR company," I said lamely.

She shook her head. "That's just my cover. What we do here is secret."

"You're what, like a valkyrie James Bond?"

"Not exactly. Counter-intelligence is part of our mission, but not the main focus."

"What is your mission?" This was too weird. First Kiki, and now Alviya? I was starting to think I didn't know any of my friends at all.

"I think it's best if Director Broussard explains everything. Then we can talk more later."

"Director—wait, Cyriaque Broussard?" The

Rougarou werewolf was an old friend of my dad's and had been around a lot when I was a kid.

"He took over as Director after your dad died."

Disbelief filled me. Cyriaque was in on this too? It was like the whole world was conspiring against me, all so sure I couldn't be trusted.

"Does Bas know what you really do?" I asked.

Alviya examined her fingernails. "Actually, Bas works here too. That's how we met."

I would have thrown up my hands if they hadn't been chained to the bed. "What the fuck, Alviya?! You're all just, what, laughing behind my back about what an idiot I was because I didn't know your big secret?"

"Of course not." Alviya grabbed my hand and I hissed. She pulled back, remorse written across her pretty features. "I wanted to tell you a thousand times, we all did. But our work here is top secret clearance only. Your dad recruited me after I became your roommate. Kiki too, although she'd already been here a few years when I joined. I met Bas here. Cyriaque and your father started this place. It wasn't purposeful; it just unfolded like that. You were so busy in med school..."

"That what, I wouldn't notice that everyone in my life was a fucking liar sneaking around behind my back?" I closed my eyes, fighting tears.

"Your dad didn't want you worrying—"

"You don't get to talk about him. None of you do.

He should have told me. He robbed me of this whole...piece of himself. And now I feel like maybe I never really knew him at all." Dad had been my person. And I had been his. Or so I'd thought.

"You knew him. You knew how much he loved you."

I closed my eyes. "I think I'm ready to yell at Cyriaque now. If you can unchain me."

When I finally looked at her, tears shimmered in the corner of Alviya's obsidian eyes. "I'm so, so sorry Zariya. Please forgive me."

"Just get these fucking things off me."

ALVIYA LED me silently through the base. We passed a few rooms of interest: a dining hall where supes were sitting around a table and eating as well as a wide training room where two women sparred. I did my best to ignore it. My focus was on my anger. My rage.

Alviya knocked on the door and it opened to reveal Konstantin Bauer, filling the doorway in a black leather jacket and jeans. My breath caught in my throat, as if the air had been sucked out of the room by his mere presence.

"Zariya." He nodded, stepping out of the way and crossing his arms across his broad chest. "Created quite a mess down on the fifth floor."

"You can blame your dragon pet for that," I said. "I was just looking for some answers." I thought of the file I'd found with Dad's records. Who knew where that had gone in all this mess?

"And it's time you got some." Cyriaque came around his desk and waved a hand, ushering me inside his office. I crossed my arms. He better not be bullshitting me.

Alviya gave me a weak smile and walked down the hallway with Konstantin, leaving the two of us alone.

Cyriaque looked just as he had the last time I'd seen him—at my father's funeral. Tall and devilishly good-looking, with thick, chestnut hair and a full beard. His black Armani suit had been exchanged for a white button-down and slacks today, and he wore the sleeves rolled up, revealing strong forearms. I had a hard time reconciling this serious character with the man who'd played Marco Polo with me for hours at the community pool when I was eight.

"Have a seat, Zariya," he said with his southern drawl, settling down into his own chair. I wanted to be difficult and stand, but I was still feeling a little woozy from the tranquilizers, so I sank into the leather chair across his desk.

"I'm sorry you had to find out this way."

"You mean you're sorry I found out at all?" Clearly, me finding out hadn't been the plan.

He sighed. "How about we start at the beginning.

You must have lots of questions. I'm happy to answer them."

"What the hell is this place?"

"This is Tartarus Base, the home of Veil Force. We're a covert, black-ops division of MASC. I report directly to the MASC Undersecretary myself."

"So all this time, when I thought Dad was a diplomat for MASC, he was what, a spy? An assassin? A special operator?" I guess I could see Dad in those roles, but I still couldn't believe that he wouldn't tell me. That he'd have this whole other life and lie about it.

"We are whatever MASC needs us to be. Our mission is to protect humans and supes alike from magical and supernatural threats. We investigate and stop terrorist threats, capture or eliminate individuals who have been deemed to be a danger to supernatural security around the globe, find and neutralize hazardous magical items...the list goes on. Our missive is flexible, because the threats are ever-changing."

"So you're like a supernatural global police force?"

"Of a sort. But we don't spend our time enforcing laws. Much of what we do operates in areas where there is no law."

"And Dad was the Director?" I said in disbelief.

"Your father and I started Veil Force. He was a team leader, and then Director for the last decade.

When we served in the Marines, we realized that human military and counter-intelligence groups weren't equipped to handle many magical and supernatural threats. And, unfortunately, due to prejudices, ensuring supe safety and rights around the world was not a top priority. We pitched Veil Force to the Security Council, and they went for it. Our group is classified, as we've found much of our work is more easily done in the shadows. Not to mention humans still get nervous knowing that teams of powerful supes are running around beneath their noses. But our existence is known to a select few— we do collaborate with various UN and foreign government agencies on some missions."

That was all well and good. This place couldn't have been more like Dad if his picture had been on the damn brochure. But that wasn't what I really wanted to know. "Why didn't he tell me?"

Cyriaque cocked his head, his brown eyes kind. "You were seven years old when we started to build this place. It wasn't appropriate to discuss it with you and your father didn't want you worrying about him. You were all each other had, other than Temsula."

"Still, he should have told me when I got older."

"He worried. That if he did, it would put you at risk. Or that you'd want to join. He wanted you to follow your dreams, not his."

"A lot of good that did. My dreams have gone to

shit," I muttered, guilt needling at me. After all the work I'd put into med school, I'd ruined it.

"I know. I'm sorry."

I crossed my arms over my chest, examining his office. Looking everywhere but at his sympathetic face. The framed photo of him and my dad. An ancient jeweled dagger in a glass box. A watercolor painting of a dark wolf silhouetted against a smoky sunset.

"How many of you are there?"

"We have four teams of six—Phoenix Team is led by Konstantin Bauer, whom I understand you've met. The other teams are Aquila, Hydra, and Draco. I led Draco team until your father...well, until I took this job. Then we have a few base support staff like Oliver and Kimiko. A few more."

"I want to know about Dad's death. Kiki gave me a fake report, didn't she?"

Cyriaque leaned forward, running his hands through his hair. "I'm afraid that was my idea, Zariya. I knew you would be like a dog with a bone if you got wind of foul play surrounding your father's death, and frankly, I didn't want that for you. He wouldn't have, either. Vizol would want you living your life, not chasing after revenge."

"Well, Dad's gone, so he doesn't get a say. Tell me the truth. You owe me that much. Dad was murdered, wasn't he?"

Cyriaque's pause spoke volumes. Finally, he looked up, meeting my gaze. "Yes, we think so."

The heat of vindication flooded through me. I knew it. I *knew it*. Everyone had told me to move on, that I'd been imagining things. But I knew that Dad hadn't died in some freak accident. "Do you know who did it?"

"Not yet. Believe me when I say we are all working on it. Everyone here loved Vizol; he personally recruited most of our team. We will find who did this, Zariya, and we will make them pay."

"I want to be involved," I said.

"I thought you'd might say that. But this is Veil Force business. We'll handle it."

Bullshit. They weren't cutting me out of this. "Then I'm joining."

"I thought you might say that too."

"I'm just as tough as anyone out there. I've been fighting for two decades. I'm a naga. We're warriors by nature. You owe me this, Cyriaque, you can't keep me out. Not any longer—"

"Easy, girl." He held up his hands. "Even if I wanted to deny you a place, that burn on your hand says otherwise."

I'd forgotten. I looked down at the mark on my palm and my eyes widened. Cyriaque held up his palm, displaying the same mark. "All of the Veil Force operators—'Phantoms,' we're called—have been marked by that sword. It chooses us. Marks us as worthy."

"I don't understand. Dad told me he was burned by some ancient sword in India."

"Not entirely accurate. Well, the India part, anyway. That sword is *Caledfwlch*, one of the legendary objects of power in Irish lore. Also known in some tales as 'Excalibur.' The sword has a long history of choosing those who are worthy to wield it. It chose your father first. And it's chosen each of us to fight beside him."

"So, what, Dad was King Arthur, and you're the Knights of the Round Table?" I offered a half-hearted joke.

He didn't laugh. "In a way. It has become the symbol of Veil Force—the sword and the shield. It's what we do, and who we are."

"But Kiki doesn't have one. Or Alviya," I pointed out.

"Most of our members have the mark healed after the sword chooses them. Some of us keep the brand. As a reminder. But whatever you decide, Zariya, that sword's choice marks you as one of us as surely as your Chanji blood does."

"Great. When do I start?" Was I really doing this? Joining some clandestine governmental organization with a secret base below New York City?

But it was one of the last pieces of Dad I had left. I couldn't just walk away from it without exploring what it meant. Plus, if I wanted to hunt down the men who had killed Dad, I needed these powerful supes at my side. And their fancy-pants resources.

"It's not so simple as that. Veil Force is an elite group. Phantoms are chosen after years in service—most have worked for counter-intelligence or in special operations."

I prickled. "I get it. You think I won't measure up."

"To the contrary. I'm sure you will. But I'm not the one who needs convincing. It's the rest of the Phantoms. The supes who'd be relying on you out in the field."

Like Konstantin Bauer. "Fine. What do I have to do to prove it to them?"

"It's funny you should ask..."

A test. I hated tests.

My head spun as I walked out of Cyriaque's office.

Cyriaque stood in his doorway. "We'll need a day to prepare. And a day of rest would do you good after tonight's...excitement. Report back here at 0600 on Monday if you want to take the test."

I ran a thumb over the burn on my palm. It throbbed, hot and angry. "I'll be here."

"I thought you'd say that."

"I want the real report."

"When you pass the test—"

"No, Cyriaque. Now. I deserve the truth, no matter whether I'm fit to join your little club or not."

Cyriaque sighed and started down the hallway, jerking his head for me to follow. "Fine. Konstantin has it."

We stopped at an office four doors down, and he poked his head inside. "Get her the real report."

I stepped inside, standing awkwardly. Cyriaque disappeared. I guessed he was done with me. Konstantin stood up from behind a large wooden desk, a pair of trendy, clear-rimmed glasses on his nose. He quickly took them off.

"Vampires wear glasses?" I couldn't help myself.

He strode past me to the filing cabinet at the back of the room, sending a whiff of his scent of cool breezes and night air my way. And giving me a good look at how his clothes clung to the muscles of his form—his broad back, his ass. My cheeks heated. *Stop staring at the vampire's ass, Chanji!*

"Vampires keep their human afflictions even after we're turned. I just need them for reading."

I ran quickly through what I knew about vampires. "So you're Derived?" I asked.

There were two types of vamps—Authentics and Derived. Authentic vampires lived in remote colonies and rarely mingled with human society. Authentic vampires had never been human—and they were the only type that could make a Derived vampire—a vampire who had once been human. Authentics also lived exclusively on blood while Deriveds could survive on a combination of human food and blood. It was why they were more easily Recognized. Authentics were Unrecognized—outside the protection of normal law, which was for the best. Because really, we needed protection from them, not the other way around. They were savage. Animal. Not members of polite society.

Konstantin inclined his head. The gesture was calculated, as if he had to remind himself to make such a typical human movement. "I am."

"When...?" I trailed off.

"1423."

Damn. He was old. I knew vampires grew in strength as they aged. I felt slightly better about the fact that he'd bested me in our sparring match.

Konstantin handed me a file from the cabinet. "The real report. I'll walk you out."

I followed him towards the elevator. "Don't trust me to find the exit on my own?"

"Just a precaution," he replied.

"You could have saved us all a lot of trouble if you'd just given me the real report when I asked for it."

"It wasn't my call."

We were at the elevator now and he pushed the button for me before turning. His expression was inscrutable. Devastating. It was hard to think when he looked at me full on like that, with those blue, blue eyes.

1423, I reminded myself. That made him... I didn't even know. If you needed a calculator to figure out a guy's age, you shouldn't be lusting after him, right? That seemed like a wise rule of thumb.

"It wasn't Kiki's call, either. Don't be too hard on her."

"Why do you care?"

"I care about everyone here. Veil Force...what your father built here...we're a family. We take care of our own."

His words were a gut punch.

"Understood," I managed. I stepped into the elevator quickly and hit the button for the ground floor. I willed the elevator doors to close before I started to cry. I couldn't look at him—wouldn't look at him—and when the doors finally slid shut, a sob escaped me.

I crumpled to my knees, the folder pressed to my chest, one hand clapped over my mouth.

What your father built here...we're a family. The truth of it hit me like a semi-truck. It had always been Dad, Auntie, and me—they'd been the only family I'd had. But Dad had built a whole other family in secret, behind my back. Without me. All his business trips and travel took on new form in my memories. Dad hadn't been committed to his job; he'd been committed to his other life. The family he preferred over me.

I rose and screamed, punching the elevator door with my fist. My strike left a circular dent, and the pain startled away my tears. My chest heaved as the doors opened into the little alcove that would take me through the portal back to Four Freedoms Park.

Fewer than four hours had passed since I'd gone down this very elevator, but it felt like years. The weight of sorrow clung to me like an anchor. I felt worse than I had when Dad had died. I wanted to curl up in a corner of the concrete space and succumb to the blackness of sleep, but there was something else I needed to do. Someone else I needed to yell at. So I stepped through the portal and headed for a cab.

Auntie Temsula lived in a quirky Victorian in Montclair, New Jersey. She loved America, but she'd never liked the big city. Even New Jersey was busier than she liked, but she'd wanted to be close to us.

Everything about Auntie was as quirky as her home. She made her living as a psychic and a medium and was a damn good one at that. But right now I couldn't think about anything except that she *had* to have known about Veil Force. About Dad's secret MASC dealings and his other family. And she'd kept it from me too.

It was just after 3 A.M. by the time I arrived, but I didn't care. I banged on the front door and shouted her name. "Auntie! Wake up!"

I was about to bang again when she pulled the door open, a colorful floral robe haphazardly wrapped around her. "Curlicue? What's wrong? What's happened?"

I stormed past her into the foyer, rounding on her. I held up my burnt hand, showing her the brand. "We need to talk."

She stumbled back a step, her hand flying to her mouth. She recovered quickly, closing the door. "I'll make some chai. And I'll tell you whatever you want to know."

I wanted to yell at her to tell me now, but damn it if some of Auntie's chai didn't sound fucking delicious. So I led the way into the kitchen, dropping down into one of the chairs tucked into the island. The ceiling of her kitchen was painted like an Indian sunrise, and the cabinets each had mismatching hardware. Every corner and open space of her house was filled with color—carvings and wall-hangings, clustered altars to the gods. I felt my roiling anger draining away, leaving me spent and empty.

"You want an ice pack for that burn?" Auntie asked.

I nodded sullenly and took it, pressing it to my hand with a sigh. I thought Dr. Dragon back at the base had put some sort of salve on it, because my hand smelled faintly of camphor and hadn't been throbbing as badly as I would have expected. But still, the ice felt heavenly.

Auntie poured coconut milk into a pan on the

stove, her back to me. "Why don't you tell me what's happened?"

So I did. Woodenly, I recited the events of the evening. Grappling with Kiki and shooting her with the memory serum, stealing her ring and breaking into Tartarus base, the dragon, the sword. Talking to Cyriaque and the test.

Auntie turned to me, her arms crossed before her. She didn't look a day over thirty, her black, curly hair wild around her shoulders. She was beautiful, her naga heritage hidden in her human form. I envied her—that she could pass as human. Whereas I actually *was* half-human and would always look *other*.

"Do you remember the Arcana Prep bombing?" she asked.

I blinked. That wasn't what I'd expected. How could I not? I'd been six years old, and we'd been here in this very kitchen, with the news on in the background. The image on the screen was burned in my memory—the bodies of children blackened and twisted. The news anchor explained in sober tones the details of the terrorist bombing that had ripped apart a private school—a school for children of supernatural creatures. One of those little bodies had had wings, another hooves. They'd been too far gone to see what type of supes they had been, but as I stroked the scales running down my neck, I knew it could have been me. I remembered Dad's fury, burning so hot, it scared me almost as much as the images on the screen. Auntie had taken me in her arms and rocked me until I stopped crying, her own tears mingling with mine. "Of course I do."

"That was the catalyst for Veil Force. Your father knew that things like that would keep happening unless someone did something. Unless someone cared. So he and Cyriaque started their campaign to the MASC Under-Secretary. Through sheer force of will, they secured the funding and approvals to start the project. It is his greatest legacy. Besides you, of course."

"Why didn't he tell me?"

"When it began, you were a child. And as you got older...he worried if you knew, you'd want to join. You always idolized him, wanted to do everything he did. And he didn't want that life for you."

"He was my dad. Of course I fucking idolized him!" Dad had always been like a superhero to me, ever since I'd been a little girl—strong, capable, commanding. I supposed he'd had the double-life thing down, too.

"You were doing so well in medical school—you'd found your own path—"

"He should have told me."

She sighed and turned to stir the chai. "Yes, he should have. For now through his lies, he's brought to pass the very thing he wanted to prevent."

"Did he think I wouldn't be good enough?" My voice broke.

Auntie whirled and crossed the kitchen in a blink, laying her hand on my cheek. "No, curlicue. He knew you would be too good."

I blinked back tears. "What do you mean?"

"You're a naga, and a Chanji what's more. You have battle in your blood. It sings to you, calls you to challenge and fight. That's why he put you in training when you were so young—he hoped to channel it. He wanted a normal life for you. An American life. A life like your mother should have had. Marriage. Children. Peace. A Veil Force Phantom has none of these."

"Dad made it work. He had me."

"But he didn't have peace. He constantly worried he wasn't a good enough father to you, that he wasn't here enough. And he worried when he was home that he wasn't giving his teams all they deserved. He was a man pulled in half, with one foot in two worlds."

"I know the feeling," I grumbled, running my tongue over my soft fangs, retracted in my mouth. I would never be fully human, or fully naga.

Auntie poured me a big mug of chai and placed it before me. "I am sorry for the lies. And I know he is too."

I gazed into the caramel swirl of the liquid. "I just

feel…" I cleared my throat. "Like he wanted a different family. Like I wasn't enough."

"Nothing could be further from the truth." Auntie stilled, her hands braced on the cerulean tiles of the counter.

"Auntie?"

"Hold on a moment, curlicue." She disappeared into the hallway, leaving me to salve my raw wounds with the sweet spice of chai tea.

She returned a moment later, a long, black case in her hand. She set it on the counter before me, her hands on its lid as if to keep it from springing open. "Before he died, your father left this with me. He wanted you to have it, but only if you someday learned about his work with Veil Force."

Curiosity overcame my hurt. "What is it?"

Auntie unclasped the brass buckles and opened it for me.

I gasped. "Dad's talwar?"

It was a sword, a beautiful curving blade of shining silver. The hilt was wrapped in fine red leather, inlaid with gold, and etched with carvings of sinuous snakes. I'd only seen it a few times as a child —Dad had kept it under lock and key. The ornately detailed scabbard lay next to it in the case, both nestled in the black velvet.

"It's a family heirloom, passed to him by his father, and his father before that. Generations of Chanji warriors have wielded this blade."

I reached for it eagerly.

"Zariya—" Auntie held up her hand. "This blade is enchanted with strong magic. Do you smell it?"

I opened my glands and breathed deeply. Now that she pointed it out, I did—the loamy soil scent of ancestor magic. Earth and roots and old, ancient things. "What's the spell?"

"I do not know. But I suspect if you take up this blade, there will be no going back."

Good. I had nothing to go back to.

I seized the sword's hilt. And the world dropped away.

13

———

I stood in a dark room—a cavern of sorts. Yet not. It had no smell, no heat or cold—no dust or dank or dirt. It did, however, have another person.

When he turned around, my knees nearly buckled. "Dad?" I blinked and blinked again, disbelieving what I was seeing. But he was here.

I ran to him and threw myself into his arms, but instead of hitting the solid bulk of him, I stumbled through and out the other side. I fell to my knees hard, but it didn't hurt. No pain here, either. I held up my hand and found it ghostly and incorporeal. No body at all.

I turned, shoving to my feet. "Dad?" My voice wavered. "Where are we? What is this place?"

"This is my memory palace," he said. "I created it

in case you ever needed my knowledge. The knowledge of your ancestors."

I shook my head. "What? How—"

"The Balsamic Moon coven specializes in memories and mind magic. A powerful witch owed me a favor, and this is what I asked of her." The North American witches were divided into eight main covens, named after the phases of the moon. The covens differed widely in philosophy, approach to magic, and their approach to flouting the laws. The Balsamic witches were considered to be on the "not evil" end of the spectrum.

"Why?" In its shock, my brain was moving like molasses.

"Because I knew a time might come when you'd want to follow in my footsteps. And if I was no longer around—I still wanted you to have my wisdom."

"You knew I might want to join Veil Force."

"Of course, my darling. How could you not? You are fierce and brave and detest injustice. Veil Force was made for supes like you."

"But you lied to me about it! If you thought I'd be so great at it, why didn't you tell me?"

"Because in my selfishness, I did not want you at risk."

I was temporarily stunned. Tears pricked my eyes. Great. Of course there were tears in this place. "That's a shit reason."

"I know. But you were always my greatest treasure."

"How can you say that when you spent your life building a secret base, a whole secret family?"

"I can only ask forgiveness for how I've wronged you. I did what I thought was best. I only ever wanted your happiness and safety."

"I was happiest with you," I managed to choke through the tears. I threw up my hands. "Why am I even arguing with you? What are you, a figment of some witch's imagination? You're dead."

"I am a fragment of your father's consciousness. Left here to guide you through the memories available."

I pressed my lips together. "So you're really...him? A piece of him?"

"The only piece left, it seems."

I wrapped my arms around myself, struggling to hold it together. Seeing him—it should be better, to have even the smallest piece of him right here before me. But it wasn't. It was worse. He was here, but I couldn't touch him, I couldn't hug him or pound my fists into his chest for what he'd done. It just reminded me of how much I'd lost. "I want to go now."

"Very well," Dad's form said, unperturbed. "If you ever wish to return, you have only to touch the sword and ask for a memory. I will supply it to you."

And then I was back, blinking away the light of

Auntie's kitchen, my hand closed around the buttery leather of the talwar's hilt. She hadn't moved an inch. It was like I'd never been gone.

I dropped the sword back into the case like I'd been burned.

Auntie was there, her hand on my shoulder, her green eyes searching. "Are you all right?"

All I could do was shake my head as the tears poured forth. She wrapped me in her arms as I sobbed, feeling like I'd lost him all over again.

I THOUGHT I'd already reached the bottom of my well of my grief, but I'd been wrong. It went deeper than I knew—miles of dark and cold.

Auntie held me as I cried that night, her own tears perfuming my hair as we spooned in her big four-poster bed. The sun was rising when I finally fell into a fitful sleep.

I woke exhausted, my head tight and pounding, my heart rung dry.

She fed me coffee in the morning with dosa bread smeared with fig jam and ricotta cheese.

The folder sat on the countertop, next to the tightly closed case bearing the sword. I'd forgotten all about it. So I opened it and read while I ate.

"What is that?"

"The report on Dad's death," I admitted.

Auntie froze for a moment in the act of returning the creamer to the fridge but then recovered. "What does it say?"

I scanned it with a strange mix of eagerness and trepidation. "They found evidence of magical charges on the pillars of the building Dad drove by—C4 explosives with a spelled trigger. They said it looks like Black Moon Coven technology, but they're still investigating." The Black Moon Coven had been officially declared a terrorist organization by MASC two years back.

"So he was killed on purpose. You always said."

"You're the one who taught me to follow my intuition," I retorted.

"There's that sass. You must be feeling better." A ghost of a smile crossed Auntie's face. "I should have listened."

"It's okay. I get why you didn't want to believe me. *I* didn't really want to believe me."

"Any other clues?"

I finished scanning the report. "Just one. They discovered a strange circle imbedded on the concrete behind the facade that collapsed. Large—as if the stone had been imprinted upon, but the imprint was raised. Markings of some kind. Lettering? Runes? I can't make it out." I showed her the grainy black-and-white photo in the report.

We both peered at it, our heads together, as if getting closer to the image would make it reveal its secrets. "I have never seen its like," Auntie finally said. "You make them show you the details of these markings. We will find whatever magic did this."

"I will. If I pass, that is." My stomach flipped. The test would start tomorrow at 6 A.M. What had I gotten myself into?

"You will. You have your father's memories to aid you." My eyes flicked to the black case. It was beyond weird to think that I could access Dad's memories whenever I wanted. I was torn between desperate curiosity and my low-burning anger at him. "I'm not ready to go back in."

"Then you have friends who can help prepare you."

"I'm not asking Kiki or Alviya for help. I don't even want to see them."

Auntie clucked her tongue. "I know you're angry, but what did your father always say?"

I pursed my lips. "Use every resource at your disposal."

"There are times in life when the line between ally and enemy becomes blurred. In those moments, practicality must govern, not emotion."

"Thanks, Sun Tzu," I muttered. "I never thought I'd hear you advocating logic over emotion."

"We have both for a reason, curlicue. And I am still a naga. We keep to the three-fold path."

"I know."

For a second, I could see Dad in front of me. I was

small, and he was down on one knee. I'd just gotten the crap kicked out of me by two human kids who lived three houses up, and green blood dribbled from my nose. He was wearing his fatigues, back before he'd started wearing business suits instead. When I sobbed at him that I wanted to learn to fight, he shook his head calmly and asked, "Do you think muscles make you strong? Training?" I nodded, wiping the back of my hand across my nose. He shook his head gently and poked me in the belly. "Nagas know that strength comes not from might, but from here. Your intuition. Let it guide you." He poked me gently in the breastbone. "Here. Your heart. Where courage and compassion lie. Let it guide you." He poked me between the eyes. "And here. Wisdom. Let it guide you. This is the three-fold path. Let it guide you, and you will always have what you need."

Tears pricked my eyes and I shoved them down. I wanted to scream at him, to flail against his memory. *I don't have everything I need, do I, Dad? Because you're gone.*

But as much as I felt wrung out and raw, I knew Auntie was right. I needed an edge if I wanted to pass whatever test they were planning for me. Using Dad's memories was the smart play, but I didn't know if I could see him again without falling apart. Kiki and Alviya were my other option. I didn't want to face them, either, though; I was still so furious about their lies.

Either way, I had fewer than twenty-four hours to decide.

Just after noon, I let Auntie wrap me in a hug and hand me a bag full of fragrant leftovers and called myself and Dad's talwar an Uber. I was still angry at her, but I was beginning to see that Dad had made a decision a long time ago that had shaped all of the lives around me. I couldn't cut out everyone in my life for toeing the line he'd set. Or I'd have no one left.

I went to wait for my ride outside in the fresh spring morning, closing my eyes to bask in the sun.

That was why I didn't see the car until it was almost upon me. Tires squealed and my eyes flew open to reveal a black SUV with tinted windows skidding to a stop directly in front of me.

Four black-clad soldiers with face masks and assault rifles burst from the car. Coming at me. Coming *for* me? Either way, it couldn't be good.

I launched into a run, sprinting down the street.

Something hit me from behind, square between my shoulder blades. I went down—hard. My chin scraped against the pavement, taking the brunt of my fall.

My lungs rebelled against me, unwilling to pull in breath. Had I been shot?

I hazarded a look over my shoulder.

Two sets of black-booted legs were approaching —their steps tight and precise.

I tried to push up to my hands and knees, but my muscles were frozen. Weak. Another tranq dart? Auntie's food had spilled over the sidewalk before me, and the case for Dad's sword had busted open. The talwar was lying just a foot from me. If I could reach it...

The men were almost upon me.

I rallied every last drop of energy and lunged forward. My hands connected with the hilt. And I was whisked away.

14

The memory palace was just as it had been. Dad stood calmly across the stone space, regarding me.

I, on the other hand, was freaking the fuck out.

I'd come in on hands and knees—I pushed to my feet. "Dad, someone's attacking me."

He frowned. "I'm sorry to hear that."

I growled. "That's it? You're sorry?" Where was Dad's fire? His righteous fury?

"The fragment that was preserved does not include emotion. But perhaps I can help you another way?"

Yes. I needed help. "Memories."

"What would you like to know?"

I didn't know what the hell was going on, or who the hell these people were. All I knew was that I was splayed out on the sidewalk like old take-out and when I returned to my body from the strange time of this place, I'd probably be loaded into that car. Or killed. Or loaded into the car and then killed. This might be my only chance to learn what Dad knew. To benefit from his wisdom. "Everything. Show me everything."

Dad shook his head. "That's unadvisable. The weight of that many memories being added to your neural pathways at one time—it could overload your circuits, so to speak."

"I might not have any circuits left to overload if we don't do this. Give me the memories. Now."

He clucked his tongue. "Very well." He stepped in close, looking so much like Dad that it made my heart seize. The green of his eyes, the flecks of gray at his temples, the strength and authority that radiated from him...

He held out his hand, as if to shake mine.

"I thought I couldn't touch you."

"You may only during the transfer."

So I threw my arms around him. He was solid and real and *Dad*.

Then the onslaught began.

I CAME to in some sort of warehouse. Cold concrete floor beneath me, a tall ceiling with dim, buzzing lights above. Someone had hung plastic to section the space off into a sort of macabre room. Horror movie chic.

I took in the space, catalogued what I knew. Tried to ignore the fact that I was chained to a chair. That my chin smarted like hell from where I'd smacked it on the pavement.

My head felt like it might split apart from the weight of new knowledge. I didn't know if this was what it felt like to have my circuits overloaded, but I suspected it might. It was like there were two people inside me.

Zariya, who was practically peeing her pants in terror right now. I'd been *kidnapped*.

And there was Vizol. Calm. In control. He'd gotten out of situations ten times worse than this without breaking a sweat. Was this how Dad had felt all the time, supremely confident and sure of his own abilities? It was a heady feeling, especially compared to the stress ball of doubts and insecurities that was Zariya.

But Dad's fearlessness had gotten him killed. He hadn't been invincible, and neither was I.

I desperately wanted to explore my new knowledge, to swim through the waters of Dad's memories like a fish. Flashes of his memories of me surfaced— me with pigtails and a gap in my smile, me flying a kite on the seashore with a look of pure childhood delight on my face. I could feel his love for me. His pride. It was like oxygen to my suffocating heart.

I'd thought Dad had wanted another family because I hadn't been enough. I knew now how wrong I'd been. He'd built Veil Force *because* of me. Because other supes deserved safety too. Lives where their children could grow up and join the world as equals.

A man in black military gear slipped under the plastic, startling me out of Dad's memories.

I gave myself a mental kick. I should have finished analyzing my predicament, not taken a stroll down memory lane.

The man dragged a chair across the cement floor, dropped it across from where I sat, and settled into it. He was tall and muscular, with a chiseled, handsome face and chocolate-brown hair cut short. Though he looked human, he moved with a preternatural grace that cried *supe*. I wondered what he was. I didn't recognize him from any of Dad's memories.

I opened my glands and quested out to see what was around. The building was large, with six bodies within. It must have been located in a fairly deserted area, though, because I couldn't make out any other people or supes nearby. The building smelled faintly of oil and gasoline. So some sort of auto storage or repair facility. That was helpful but didn't exactly narrow the location down. That could put us in any one of a thousand places in the Tri-State area.

The supe in black was examining me, one booted

foot resting on the other knee. His body language wasn't particularly hostile. More like curious.

The silence between us was itching at me, but Dad's memories said to stay silent. Let him take the lead. So I stared back, meeting his brown eyes.

"Zariya Chanji," he finally said.

"Gold star for you," I retorted.

I could practically feel Dad smacking his forehead in exasperation. I supposed antagonizing your enemy with futile snark was not part of the Veil Force handbook.

"I apologize for the force with which you were brought here. My men got a little...overeager. They have been disciplined."

"Who are you? Why am I here?"

"We are an organization that acquires objects of value." So...thieves. "We keep a close eye on what goes on in the supernatural law enforcement community. You came to our attention as the newest member of Veil Force."

Not if I didn't get the hell out of here and back to Tartarus base by 0600 tomorrow. "I don't know what you're talking about. I'm not a member of anything."

The man pursed his lips. "Now, Zariya, let's dispense with the facade, shall we?"

I said nothing, which I guessed he took as assent.

"We would benefit from having a woman on the inside. Someone who could help us understand where Veil Force was going to be next. Help us keep a few steps ahead."

I scoffed. This guy had a pair of *cojones* on him. "You want me to spy for you?"

"I understand it may seem distasteful, and so we're prepared to make it worth your while. Our clients pay handsomely for the items we procure for them. We would be willing to pay half a million dollars per year for you to serve as our eyes and ears inside Tartarus."

Half a million... My eyes goggled. Damn, that was a lot of money. *Corrupt, wrong, never!* Dad's memories practically shouted at me.

Well, yes, obviously, I wasn't actually going to do it. However nice a cool half a mil might have sounded. I'd never betray what Dad had built, what Veil Force stood for.

I shook my head. "No way. *If* I knew what you were talking about, and *if* I were a member, there's no amount of money that would turn me into your mole."

The man frowned, rubbing his strong jaw. "I urge you to reconsider, Zariya. You see, we will have you for our spy, one way or another. We'd prefer you to cooperate willingly. It's easier on everyone. But we're prepared to do this the hard way."

The hairs on the back of my neck rose. "You can't make me do anything."

"Unfortunately for you, that's just not true."

He stood and ducked under the plastic. My pulse roared to life, my senses on high alert. What was he doing? What was he getting?

Feeling out with my glands, I saw that he was returning with someone else. A smaller, female form. So not *what* was he getting...but whom. A supe.

I threw up my mental walls, forming them tightly around my mental space. Dad had been through serious anti-interrogation training from both human and supe adversaries, so I added his knowledge to my own, using the techniques he'd been taught to fortify my walls even stronger. Until they were as sturdy as steel. Impenetrable.

When the black-clad man reappeared, I was ready. For the woman at his side, not so much.

She was petite and lovely, clad in a suit of pink herringbone. Her platinum blonde hair cascaded in curls over her shoulders and her makeup was perfect. She looked like she belonged ruling the boardroom of a fashion empire, not in this dank place.

I wanted to laugh in relief.

But not Dad. He had known her. And for the first time since his memories had poured into my mind, a rare sensation surfaced from the depths. Fear.

15

———

Konstantin's phone rang for the second time. *Damn it.* He ignored it, pulling the pillow over his head. Didn't a man deserve a few hours of peace?

He felt a shudder against his mental shields, as if a giant were pounding on the door. That could only be Kiki. Which meant it was Kiki who was calling.

He dragged himself from bed and grabbed his phone. "What?"

Kiki sounded near tears. "Konstantin, I think you should get down here. Cyriaque...I don't know what he's thinking. This is super fucked-up."

The remaining fog in his mind cleared. "Calm down. What's going on?"

"The test Cyriaque is putting Zariya through. He called in the *mara*."

He froze. "What test? Zariya's test isn't until tomorrow."

"No. It's happening right now. They took her to some warehouse. Konstantin, she's torturing her."

"I'll be right there."

Konstantin threw on jeans and a T-shirt and was out the door, wishing the elevator from his penthouse apartment was quicker. Vampires in modern literature always had astounding powers like the ability to fly, to turn into a bat, or to run as fast as the speed of light.

The elevator doors opened to the garage, revealing the sleek lines of his Audi R8. While he did have incredible strength, speed, and stamina, if he needed to get somewhere fast, this was how he did it. He liked to think his true superpower was in having made six centuries of wise investments. The compound interest alone made him stupidly rich. As much as it galled him, in modern life, money was power. And freedom.

Konstantin shot out of the parking structure onto the streets of Manhattan. At this time in the early afternoon, traffic hadn't reached complete gridlock, and he maneuvered his way towards Four Freedoms Park.

His mind circled over what Kiki had said, again, and again. Cyriaque had told him the test was tomorrow. Had told Zariya. So what the hell was he playing at?

He shifted into high gear, the engine purring to life beneath him. He was going to fucking find out.

THE HALLWAY outside the Ops Center was filled with people—Oliver was talking with Signe and Verte in hushed tones. Alviya and Bas waited a little way down the hall, his hand on her shoulder.

When Konstantin approached, Oliver and the sisters turned to him. Verte and Signe, their two resident norns, looked nearly identical—tall, lithe blondes with bone structure a supermodel would kill for. While Signe was blind, Verte was deaf, both giving up a natural sense for the preternatural foresight their heritage had granted them. But it didn't slow either of them down—both were brilliant and an integral part of Veil Force's success.

"What's going on?" Konstantin asked.

The doors to the Ops Center were shut. Through the window, Konstantin could see that only Kiki and Cyriaque were inside.

Kiki flashed him a quick glance. Her eyes were red-rimmed.

"Cyriaque had a team pick up Zariya this afternoon," Oliver said. "Leilani's leading. Posing as an enemy of MASC to see if Zariya can be flipped." Leilani, number two on Corvus team, was a

Hawaiian kapua shapeshifter who could take any form.

Signe shook her head. "When I said test, I meant of her skills, not her loyalty. The sword chose her. She's as honorable as her father."

"Any of my team on the mission?"

"He didn't call in any Phoenix members. I bet the Director knew you wouldn't like it."

"Damn right I wouldn't like it."

"Kiki said something about the mara?" The mara was a contractor they used when they needed someone broken—a supe with the power to control nightmares. After a few hours with the mara in his head, even the toughest sonofabitch was crying to give up his secrets.

"She's working Zariya right now," Verte said. Her voice was grave.

Emotions roared to life within him—outrage and burning anger. His vision narrowed at the thought of Zariya's delicate form wracked with the pain of her worst nightmares. And there was something else, too. A fierce desire to protect her and keep her from harm. *Ours*, it snarled.

He burst through the door of the Ops Center, going for Cyriaque. He barreled into the Director, driving him back against the far wall.

Cyriaque snarled, his fangs protruding. The air around him crackled with the electricity of a barely restrained change.

Konstantin bared his fangs right back, nearly nose to nose with the supe. Cyriaque was bulkier with muscle, but Konstantin was taller—and much, much older. "This test ends now."

"Stand down, Commander." Cyriaque growled. "Or I will have you removed from duty."

"You've gone too far. This isn't what Signe meant."

Cyriaque shoved Konstantin back, off of him. His chest heaved, his eyes dark with the threat of violence. "I'm the Director of this organization. It's my call. This test is designed to ensure she is loyal to us and can withstand the psychological pressures that she would face as a Phantom."

"Her dad just died. She shouldn't have to go through this. Vizol would be turning over in his grave at this bullshit."

Cyriaque bared his teeth. "Don't lecture me on what Vizol would or wouldn't have wanted. I knew him longer than you. What Vizol would want is for us to be sure that his daughter can handle the job. Coddling her won't do her any favors."

The sound of a scream ripped through the array of computer monitors. Konstantin risked a glance. Kiki's elbows were braced on the desk, her hands covering her mouth.

"This is what you call coddling her? Sending the mara to rip apart her mind?"

"Anyone can fight, Konstantin. Anyone can

follow orders. We need more from her. We need her to be able to think her way out of an impossible situation. To face the worst and not break."

Konstantin let out a low growl, wishing he didn't see a sort of horrible sense in what Cyriaque was saying. The voice inside of him still wanted to strike out at the Director for what he was doing—put a stop to Zariya's suffering. Some part of him cared far too much.

He shoved that part down.

"I told the mara to be gentle. She's not going to turn it up to ten in there."

"Does that monster know the meaning of the word 'gentle'?" Konstantin muttered.

"Director," Kiki said. "Something's happening."

Zariya's screams had stopped. Leilani, sporting the skin of a random military-aged male, and the mara had retreated from the alcove where Zariya was chained.

"See, they're giving her a break," Cyriaque said.

Konstantin leaned in to examine the computer monitors. "What's she doing?" Zariya was frantically fiddling with the chains at her wrists.

She pulled her arms free, the chains falling to the ground. "Holy shit, she's escaping." How had she done that?

She was slipping out of the rest of her chains now. Running to the edge of the plastic sheets that had been hung, peeking out.

"Inform Leilani that she's escaping," Cyriaque told Kiki, who scowled. "Now we see how she fights."

Kiki must have followed orders because Leilani and two soldiers ran back towards Zariya. When Kiki worked communications in the Ops Center, she facilitated all communications telepathically. When she couldn't be available, using specs based on her brainwaves, Signe and Verte had rigged a similar communications device that any user could wear to stand in for her and assist a team's psychic communication. But it wasn't nearly as good as Kiki herself.

Konstantin watched as Leilani and her team faced off against Zariya. He inhaled a breath in the moment they all sized each other up. And then Zariya attacked.

She was a sight to behold, her moves executed perfectly and timed flawlessly. Strike, counter, strike —she danced in and out with the grace of a ballerina.

Silence fell in the Ops Center as the three of them watched Zariya move, watched her take down one adversary. A second.

Until she and Leilani faced off. Leilani was one of the best fighters Konstantin had ever faced, but she and Zariya appeared evenly matched.

"I thought you faced her, Konstantin," Cyriaque asked. "You didn't say she was *this* good."

"She wasn't." Had she been holding back when they'd sparred in the park? It hadn't seemed like it.

And why would she have? His curiosity grew. There was clearly more to Zariya Chanji than met the eye.

Zariya executed a roundhouse kick that dropped Leilani hard.

Konstantin winced.

She leaned in and pulled the gun from Leilani's belt, standing over her. Then pointing it at her chest.

"Cyriaque—" Konstantin said.

The gun fired. Shock bloomed through him. Leilani...one of their best operators...

"They're rubber bullets," Cyriaque said with a shaky laugh. "They're rubber bullets. I wouldn't send them in with real munitions."

Relief blasted through him like a tidal wave. Followed by anger. "This ends now, Cyriaque. Kiki, tell Zariya we're coming for her. That she can stand down."

Cyriaque didn't belay his order.

He headed for the door, but Kiki's words stopped him. "I can't reach her."

"What?" He turned.

"Her mental walls, they're rock hard. I've never felt this from her before. I don't know what's going on."

Neither did he. But somehow, Zariya had leveled up.

"Director," Kiki said, pointing to the screen. Zariya was now darting low through the warehouse, ducking behind a tall stack of black cases. The three remaining Phantoms were standing between her and the exits. "Those cases. Don't they contain real weapons?"

"Yes, they do."

"What warehouse is she at?" Konstantin asked.

"Seventeen," came Cyriaque's flat reply.

Seventeen... "Isn't that where we keep the Oblivion Charges?"

Cyriaque's tanned face had gone as white as a sheet. "Konstantin, get the hell in there. Now. Before she blows herself and our team off the face of the Earth."

16

The fight sang in my veins, a siren song of violence and vengeance. Dad's memories had shown me how to withstand the mara's nightmares, how to pick the lock on my chains.

When the black-clad men had come at me, I'd given my body over to his training, marveling as my limbs moved with a speed and a precision I'd only dreamed of.

If this was what it had felt like to be Dad, no wonder he'd been so supremely confident. I felt like I had fucking super powers.

I was holed up behind a tall pile of black crates. There were three more bad guys standing between me and freedom, but they appeared more afraid of me than I was of them. The mara had scuttled off as soon as the fighting began. Didn't want to get blood on her designer pumps, perhaps.

But before I made my break for freedom, I needed a weapon. I had the pistol I'd taken off my main interrogator, but I'd be exposed getting across the open floor to the door. I needed a distraction.

I pulled one of the cases down and crouched over it, opening the top.

Lying on a bed of black foam were four round glass balls, gleaming dully. My eyes shot open. Dad recognized these. They were called Oblivion Charges. MASC had confiscated some from a terrorist group of goblins who had planned to bomb the financial markets to up the value of their gold hordes.

I guessed there were more out there, and this terrorist group had them too. A plan was coming to life in my mind. I couldn't leave these charges here. They could be used for all manner of nefarious purposes. But the charges would level a city block. If Dad remembered correctly, I'd only have about a minute once I set the charge to get the hell out of the blast zone.

Which meant I'd need to take out the remaining tangos first. I couldn't risk getting held up when I was making my exit. I let out a little laugh. "Tangos" equaled bad guys. Even Dad's military lingo was rubbing off on me.

I peeked over the fort of crates and saw one of the

black-clad men approaching. "Stop right there!" I shouted, leveling my pistol at him.

"Zariya Chanji," he said. To my shock, he held up his hands. "I have a message from the Director. This was your test. You passed. You can now stand down."

My brows drew together. What the hell was this guy talking about? I looked around—the warehouse, the chair I'd been chained to, remembering the missing but torturous mara. No way this was MASC-approved. Cyriaque wouldn't approve something this fucked-up. Which meant this guy was playing me.

There were two doors out of here. If I could get them out of one, I could leave via the other, after I'd set the charge. I'd take the remaining three out in one blow. I licked my lips. "Fine. Each of you put your weapons down where I can see them and step outside the building. Let me have a clear path to the exit."

The soldiers seemed to be complying. They walked slowly to the center of the warehouse and dropped their pistols in a pile. Then headed for the door.

I watched them until they were out of there, then picked up one of the charges. I examined it. Dad had never actually turned one on.

But there was a pattern of symbols on it that I recognized as runes. Which one was the trigger? And then I saw the rune *Huyuluz*. Destruction.

I pressed it firmly and the clear ball bloomed to

life with glowing aquamarine light. It began a slow, blinking countdown. I set it back in the case.

Time to run.

I sprinted across the warehouse towards the other exit. I didn't know how big the blast would be, but better safe than sorry. I needed to get as far away as possible. *Sayonara, assholes*, I thought as I burst into the afternoon sun.

And barreled right into a hard body.

I tumbled to the ground but turned my momentum into a roll, coming up on one knee, my pistol pointed.

"Konstantin?" I lowered it a few inches. There was another man standing behind him, a thin twenty-something-year old with hipster glasses and a goatee.

Konstantin held up his hands. "Zariya, put the gun down. You're safe now."

I sighed and set it down, some of the tension melting away. MASC had found me. I stood. "We need to get the hell out of here—now. This place is about to blow."

Konstantin's eyes flicked to the ground, as if listening to something. Then his eyes went wide and fixed on me. "You set one of the Oblivion Charges?"

"Yes. I couldn't let these assholes have them. Who knows where they'd end up."

"These assholes are *us*! This is a MASC facility!"

"What?" If that was true, why hadn't I recognized

it from Dad's memories? Maybe he'd never actually been here.

"Leilani is still in there," the hipster guy said.

"Fuck!" Konstantin ran straight back into the building.

"Konstantin!" My mouth opened in shock. The other man disappeared before my very eyes. *What the fuck?*

I let out a scream of frustration before heading back into the building after Konstantin. All the while, common sense shouted at me. He was a vampire. He might be able to withstand a massive explosion without dying. Me, little half-naga, not so much.

Inside, the guy with the glasses was standing next to the box of crates, examining the blinking charge. How the hell had he gotten here so fast? The teal glow was blinking much faster now. We didn't have much time.

"How do you turn it off?" the guy asked.

"I don't know."

He shot me an exasperated look. "How did you turn it on?"

"I hit the *Hagalaz* rune. That one."

"So which one says *off*?"

I took it from him in shaking hands, turning it around, examining the runes. "*Dagaz* maybe? It means happiness."

I pressed it. The ball kept blinking. Well, I

supposed just because I thought not dying equated to happiness didn't mean the maker of these charges agreed.

Konstantin appeared with an unconscious female form slung over his shoulder. "What are we doing here?"

"Trying to not die!" I cried.

"If this goes off by these other charges, it will set off a chain reaction the size of a small nuclear reaction," goatee guy said.

"Who the fuck even are you?" I snapped at him.

"I'm Enigma, MASC's only teleporting warlock. And the one who will get you the fuck out of here if we can't figure this out."

Teleporting warlock? "Then why don't you teleport this glowy ball of death out of here and drop it in the ocean somewhere?" The charge was blinking even faster now. Tension climbed up my spine. I could feel our time running out.

Konstantin and Enigma looked at each other in surprise. Then Enigma grabbed the charge from me and disappeared.

He reappeared a moment later. His hair was wild, his glasses askew. He straightened the frames and cleared his throat. "Yeah, that was fucking close. Tell the Director I'm putting in for hazard pay."

"Tell him yourself," Konstantin barked. "If I see him anytime soon, I'm likely to rip his fucking throat out."

I staggered against the wall, my knees going weak as the adrenaline drained from me. I slid down to a seat on the cold floor, my face in my hands.

Konstantin transferred the unconscious woman to Enigma, who staggered a bit under her weight. "Take her to Oliver, will you?"

Enigma disappeared without a word.

Konstantin sat down beside me, his forearms resting on his knees, his head tipped back against the wall.

For a moment, we sat in silence.

"So those guys were telling the truth? This really was the test? The kidnapping? The torture? The highly deadly magical charges?" How could Cyriaque have done this to me? How could Konstantin? How could I trust any of them to be my teammates after they'd lied to me and then put me through hell like this? Was I supposed to *want* to be part of an organization that treated its own people like this?

"The Oblivion Charges weren't supposed to be part of it. That was your little improvisation."

"What was I supposed to think—"

"You did good, Chanji," he said, interrupting me.

His praise swept through me like warm sunshine, which just pissed me off even more. I didn't want to crave his approval. "This was fucked-up."

"I know." He took a breath and then let it out slowly. As if he wanted to say more but was restraining himself. "It's not what we're about. This."

He gestured to the warehouse. "Veil Force is a family." He took my branded hand and swooped a thumb across my palm, sending a delicious shiver through me. "A family you belong with. I hope you give us a chance to prove that to you."

And as angry and hurt as I was, I knew I wanted to give him that chance. Not just because I'd be able to do good at MASC and find out who'd really killed Dad. Not just because I longed to be part of the secret life my friends had built.

But because if I was being honest with myself, part of me wanted to know more of Konstantin Bauer.

It was the one reason that should keep me far away. And it was the one I knew I'd give in to.

17

Konstantin stared at the file in his hand. It was thin, just one piece of paper. A photo of Zariya Chanji stared up at him. The newest member of Phoenix Team, if Zariya forgave them for the clusterfuck that had been her test. She'd said she needed time to think about it.

He hadn't felt this anxious in centuries. Not facing down demon hordes or Nazi battalions. What would she decide?

He didn't know why she disarmed him. Was it her beauty? He'd worked with plenty of attractive females. Perhaps it was that she seemed too delicate for this work—for the coarseness of his team. Could she withstand Luiz's sullen moods, Daevin's lewd jokes? Rex's bitter diatribes, and him... Could she face the ghosts that haunted him? Far too delicate.

His fingers traced the line of her cheekbone. Far too beautiful.

But she'd passed that test, and what was more—he'd seen a strength there. The slitted eyes that stared at him were lovely, but they were something more. They were unblinking. Unyielding.

She'd faced down unknown enemies and bested one of Veil Force's most talented fighters. She'd confronted her own nightmares with hardly a blink. Her cool thinking had saved the situation. He was impressed.

But if he was honest, he knew it wasn't just that. It was the fact that Zariya had known loss and had pushed through. That was a special kind of strength.

But on the other hand, she was half-human. And he was undeniably attracted to her. Adding a woman to his team would add a layer of complication. They had enough complications already. Maybe he should insist that she join one of the other teams.

"What are you staring at, boss?" Konstantin looked up to find his second-in-command, Galu, leaning against the door frame, his tattooed arms crossed over his chest. The nereid, a form of water elemental, glided in and took the picture from him, examining it with glowing blue eyes. "Now she's a pretty fish."

"See, that. There. That's what I don't want," Konstantin said. "I don't want anyone distracted." Least of all himself.

Galu rolled his eyes, giving Konstantin a gentle punch with his webbed hand. "If you think the lot of us can't tell our ass from our elbow with a pretty face around, we've got bigger problems, right? And didn't she pass the Director's little test with flying colors? As I heard it, she got the drop on all of them."

Konstantin grunted his assent. He'd learned long ago to trust the little voice that whispered deep within him; it had never steered him wrong. But right now his inner guidance was going haywire. That voice wanted Zariya close. Needed her near. Which was exactly why he should refuse to let her join Phoenix Team, if she decided she wanted in on Veil Force. He was struggling to be rational when it came to her. "She's not even a full supe."

"I know you, boss. It's not because she's half-human and it certainly isn't because she's a woman." Galu waited calmly.

Konstantin pressed his lips together, the only sign of his displeasure. There was no hiding things from Galu. The supe navigated the waters of emotion like he'd sailed them all his life. He had to give him something. So a half-truth. "She's Vizol's daughter."

"And that's bad how? Means she's got some badass blood running in those veins."

"What if something happens to her? If I can't keep her safe..."

"From where I sit, there's no one better to look out for her than you and Phoenix. At least if she's close, you can protect her." The voice snarled within him at Galu's words. *Yes. Protect her.*

"I can't favor one of my team over the others. I need a sixth who can pull their weight equally."

Galu knocked his shoulder playfully. "We all know you favor me over the others anyway, so what's one more, am I right?"

Konstantin snorted softly.

"You already know what you'll choose, boss, so stop second-guessing. It'll make the boys nervous. They might start thinking you're not infallible."

"I'm immortal, not infallible."

"Don't let them hear you say that," Galu said with a chuckle.

Konstantin shook his head as Galu left, picking up the photo once again. There was so much of Vizol in her. "The fish is right," he muttered. "You'd want me to take care of her, wouldn't you, old friend? So that's what I'll do." The voice he could shove aside. Yes, Zariya was beautiful and there was something strangely compelling about her. But he was a professional. He could be her commander. A mentor. Nothing more.

His phone buzzed in his pocket. A text message from an unknown number. *I'm in. But you're all still on my shit list. Z.*

Konstantin couldn't stop the grin from stretching across his face.

"Look at you, all sunshine and roses. Good news?"

Konstantin looked up to find Signe striding into the room, her blonde hair streaming behind her. He struggled to check his emotions. "Chanji is in. Looks like Broussard didn't fuck it up irrevocably after all."

Signe gave him a smug little smile.

Konstantin shook his head. "You knew."

"I would be a pretty shitty demi-goddess of fate and fortune if I didn't. Timing is perfect."

"Why do you say that? You have something for us?"

"Sure do. You remember those unicorn poachers we've been tracking down? The Collectors? Well, we've got a lead. Orkney Islands. Scotland."

"Good work. When do we move out?"

"Under-secretary is still approving the mission package. Should be tomorrow."

"Good." Konstantin cocked his head. "Why are you grinning like the cat that ate the canary?"

"Satellite picked up something else on the island. A round circle, with symbols raised out of the stone."

"You're kidding. Like the circle we found where Vizol died?"

"Identical."

Now it was Konstantin's turn to smile, baring his fangs. "Looks like Zariya might get her revenge after all."

The adventure continues in PHOENIX PROTECTED...

The adventure continues in Phoenix Protected, book two of the Mythical Alliance: Phoenix Team series!

~

A craven enemy. A compelling ally. A legendary creature in danger...

Zariya Chanji agreed to join one of the Mythical Alliance's covert Special Forces teams, as it's the only way to secure a chance at revenge against the bastards that killed her father. But life on Phoenix Team is more than Zariya bargained for—from her delectable vampire commander, to her four deadly teammates who have demons of their own.

When a group of dangerous poachers called the Collectors organizes a hunt to claim the head of one of the world's most iconic mythical creatures, it's up to Phoenix Team to protect it. But the Collectors' treacherous network runs deep—perhaps even back to MASC itself. There are answers to be had if Zariya and her teammates can stay alive long enough to claim them.

Phoenix Protected is the second episode of a SERIALIZED urban fantasy tale. Approximately 30,000 words or 160 print pages. Cliffhangers ahead...

DOWNLOAD PHOENIX PROTECTED TODAY!

Warrick Mason hated unicorns.

He stood just outside the pen, peering at the three shimmering white beasts. The stallion tossed its pristine head with a scream of displeasure. He stepped in closer and it shied back, its black eyes rolling wildly.

His presence made the beasts nervous—the bony stretch of his antlers, his tall, thin form. They could sense he was a predator.

He hung his hands over the railing, his long talons clicking together.

One of the mares reared away, her pearlescent spiral horn hitting the low ceiling.

He gave her a tight smile. "You're afraid. Well, you have every right to be. This isn't going to end well for you." Unicorns were beloved by the fool humans—

some of the only supes that they cherished. Never mind that the creatures were no better than beasts, lacking in intelligence or true power. Perhaps that was why the humans liked them so much. They represented a type of magic that was safe. Controllable. Unicorns were recognized as Class H-NV. Herbivore, Non-Verbal. Just the way the humans liked it.

Well, unicorns were also worth a fucking fortune. And that was the way *he* liked it.

"Boss, I've got something on our back channel." Finn came up beside him, a laptop in his webbed hands.

"What's the word?"

"Looks like MASC is on to us. They're getting ready to spin up a mission. Contact confirmed they'll be headed our way in less than six hours," the green-haired merman said.

Warrick frowned. "Any word from the buyers for these nags?"

Finn grinned, revealing a row of shark-like teeth. "Affirmative. We have confirmation, and the wire transfer."

"What did they end up buying?"

"Only the horns. They said we can do what we want with the rest."

Warrick turned back to the pen with a grim smile, his cavernous stomach letting out a low growl.

Looked like he'd be eating well this afternoon. "Let's leave a surprise for MASC."

"What kind of surprise?"

"The exploding kind." Then he launched himself over the fence, his talons outstretched.

DOWNLOAD PHOENIX PROTECTED TODAY!

FROM THE AUTHOR

Thank you so much for taking the time to read *Phoenix Selected*! I hope you've enjoyed reading about Zariya's adventures as much as I've enjoyed writing them!

Reader reviews are incredibly important to indie authors like me, and so it would mean the world to me if you took a few minutes to leave an honest review wherever you buy books online. It doesn't have to be much; a few words can make the difference in helping a future reader decide to give the book a chance.

If you're interested in receiving updates, participating in giveaways, and requesting advanced copies of upcoming books, sign up for my mailing list at http://claireluana.com.

As a thank you for signing up, you will receive a free ebook!

ABOUT THE AUTHOR

Claire Luana grew up in Seattle reading everything she could get her hands on and writing every chance she could. Eventually, adulthood won out, and she turned her writing talents to more scholarly pursuits, going to work as a commercial litigation attorney. But it turns out that's not nearly as much fun!

Since returning to her more creative roots, Claire has written and published five fantasy series: The Moonburner Cycle, The Confectioner Chronicles, The Mythical Alliance, The Knights of Caerleon, co-written with Jesikah Sundin, and The Faerie Race, co-written with J.A. Armitage.

She lives in Seattle, Washington with her husband and two dogs. In her (little) remaining spare time, she loves to hike, travel, binge-watch CW shows, and of course, fall into a good book.

Connect with Claire Luana online at:
http://claireluana.com

OTHER BOOKS BY CLAIRE LUANA

Moonburner Cycle

Moonburner, Book One

Sunburner, Book Two

Starburner, Book Three

Burning Fate, Prequel Novella

Moonburner Cycle, Box Set

Confectioner Chronicles

The Confectioner's Guild, Book One

The Confectioner's Coup, Book Two

The Confectioner's Truth, Book Three

The Confectioner's Exile, Prequel Novella

Confectioner Chronicles, Box Set

The Knights of Caerleon, with Jesikah Sundin

The Fifth Knight, Book One

The Third Curse, Book Two

The First Gwenevere, Book Three

Gwenevere's Knights, Box Set

The Faerie Race, with J.A. Armitage

The Sorcery Trial, Book One

The Elemental Trial, Book Two

The Doomsday Trial, Book Three

The Faerie Race, Box Set

The Mythical Alliance: Phoenix Team

Phoenix Selected, Book One

Phoenix Protected, Book Two

Phoenix Captured, Book Three

Phoenix Trafficked, Book Four

Phoenix Revealed, Book Five

Phoenix Betrayed, Book Six

Mythical Alliance: Phoenix Team, Box Set

Orion's Kiss